"*From Ant to Eagle* is absolutely terrific. I was very moved and many elements of the story—the cancer crumble, beliefs about life and death, the nature of palliative care, the role of nurses, physicians, and the patients themselves in the oncology wheel—were not only riveting but informative."

— Paulette Bourgeois, Author

"I was prepared for *From Ant to Eagle* to be a 'sad' book, but to describe this book with just one emotion would be doing this extraordinary debut author a disservice. This is a book about fear, joy, frustration, acceptance, forgiveness, anger and, above all, love. This is a story of emotional truth that is sure to captivate readers of all ages."

— Ashley Spires, Author and Illustrator of The Most Magnificent Thing

"*From Ant to Eagle* is a wonderful conflation of heart, intelligence, and seriously skillful storytelling."

— Andrew Norriss, Author of Friends for Life and Jessica's Ghost

"In a clear, compelling voice, Calvin Sinclair tells the story of his quirky little brother's fight with cancer and the tremors that shake his whole family. Avoiding sentimentality or easy answers, *From Ant to Eagle* explores the complex emotions of a family on the verge of 'the cancer crumble' with stark honesty and warm compassion."

— Beth Cooley, Author of Ostrich Eye and Shelter

"A poignant story about love, loss, family and friendships that will tug at your heartstrings long after you close the book."

— Darlene Foster, Author of the Amanda Travels series

"*From Ant to Eagle* is a masterpiece. August (*Wonder*) and Melody (*Out of My Mind*) will now be in good company with Cal."

— Connie Halpern, Mrs. Figs' Bookworm, California

ALEX LYTTLE

2017

Cover Design: Michelle Halket

Published by Central Avenue Publishing, an imprint of Central Avenue Marketing Ltd.
www.centralavenuepublishing.com

Published in Canada. Printed in United States of America on acid free paper.

Library and Archives Canada Cataloguing in Publication

Lyttle, Alex, author
From ant to eagle / Alex Lyttle.

Issued in print and electronic formats.
ISBN 978-1-77168-111-7 (paperback).--ISBN 978-1-77168-112-4 (epub).--
ISBN 978-1-77168-113-1 (mobi)

I. Title.

PS8623.Y88F76 2017 C813'.6 C2016-906577-4
C2016-906578-2

In memory of my friend, Darren Bishop.

CHAPTER 1

My name is Calvin Sinclair, I'm eleven years old, and this is a story about my brother.

I wanted to start at the beginning—the day Sammy was born—but I can't remember the day he was born and anyway, I can't start there.

There's only one place I can.

Last summer.

Before the Ontario heat began to smoulder, before the corn was much higher than my knees, before I'd ever met a girl named Aleta Alvarado.

Before everything fell apart.

Let me get two things straight before I begin:

First—I loved my brother. I loved him more than I knew and more than I knew how to show. Sure, I picked on him, manipulated him, excluded him, neglected him, but deep down, I loved him. It's hard to explain, so I'll just leave it at that.

Second—and this is the hardest part to write, but it needs to be said.

I'm the one who killed Sammy.

CHAPTER 2

Our family had moved two years before to Huxbury, a small town an hour away from London, Ontario. I'm always sure to add 'Ontario' because if I only say London everyone assumes England.

That's not quite right; we didn't move to Huxbury.

We moved to the outskirts of Huxbury.

Even the small town of Huxbury with its single strip of run-down stores wasn't rustic enough for my parents. No, they were set on moving us straight to the boonies.

So I was plucked from my modern home in the middle of London and plopped down in an old, yellow-brick farmhouse in the middle of nowhere. No chance for discussion or argument, just, "Pack your stuff, Cal, we're moving to the middle of nowhere."

My street, my school, my friends—all gone. The only kid within a ten-kilometre radius was my brother, Sammy, and he was only six.

Worse, Sammy actually seemed to like the country.

He'd say things like, "Dad says the fresh air is good for us," or "Mom says we're lucky because the country is the most beautifulest place on earth."

Blah, blah, blah.

To me, beautiful would have been movie theatres and fast food, not endless cornfields and dirt roads. We didn't even have a TV!

Yep, life in the country was the crust. A twenty-four hour babysitting job that didn't pay. So I found ways to make life a little more entertaining.

Take, for example, Operation Bee Elimination.

It was a hot July day and I watched as my younger brother trudged through the garden by the side of our house dressed in his winter gear: snow pants, jacket, goggles, knit facemask, gloves, hat. I was sweating just watching.

"Cal, are you sure we shouldn't wait for Mom and Dad to get home? Maybe they know how to get rid of the bees."

Sammy was right—they probably did know. But that wasn't fun. And besides, I wasn't putting myself in any danger.

"Stop worrying! You've got your Bee Proof Suit on!" I yelled back. "Mom and Dad will be happy we got rid of the hive."

Sammy didn't look very convinced. His big, brown eyes were nervous and pleading beneath his goggles. He wanted me to tell him the mission was over. He wanted me to tell him we could wait. Instead I pointed at the wall where the hive was and gave a quick nod.

His shoulders slumped and he turned back around. "Okay, but I still don't get why you don't have to help."

"I am helping, dummy. I'm going to wait inside the screen door, ready to open it when you come running so that it's a quick get-away."

Sammy stopped arguing and continued to wade into Mom's flower garden by the side of the house.

The wasps had been bad that summer—really bad—so we'd got it in our heads to follow one long enough to find the nest. A small hole in the foundation of our old farmhouse must have been the entrance to a massive hive because wasps were constantly coming in and out. Mom and Dad had driven into the city for the day so we'd taken it upon ourselves to get rid of the nest.

"Okay, you got the bee spray?" I asked.

Sammy held up the can of WD40 we'd found in the garage. It had a small, straw-like tube at the end that was perfect for spraying into the hole. Sure, it was just oil, I knew that, but it had to do something.

"All right, commence Operation Bee Elimination," I yelled in my deepest, most serious voice.

"Okay, here goes, I guess," Sammy replied.

At first things went pretty smoothly. He sprayed the hole for at least a minute before the initial wave of wasps hit.

I saw him take a hesitant step back.

"Get in there, they can't sting you!" I yelled.

"These goggles are foggy, I can't see!"

"Keep spraying!"

If there's one skill I was blessed with, it was getting my brother to do anything. He stepped back into the cloud of wasps and continued spraying. Soon the buzzing noise was so loud I could hear it from where I stood, twenty feet away. Sammy kept spraying for a few seconds before—

"Oww! They're stinging me!" His shrill voice pierced the hum of the wasps.

My heart jumped.

Sammy never cried unless he was actually hurt.

He dropped the can and bolted toward the screen door.

Oh crust.

The wasps swarmed thickly around him, so I locked the door.

He fumbled with the handle, struggling with his winter gloves. It took a few seconds for him to realize it was locked.

"Open the door!" he wailed.

Through the thick fog in his goggles, I saw his eyes start to tear. He banged at the door but I didn't let him in. I couldn't. They would have stuck me like a pincushion.

"Run around, run around! They can't get you when you're running!" I yelled.

"They're stinging my arms!"

By now Sammy was hysterical and not listening. He fell defeated and sobbing by the foot of the door and it took nearly ten minutes for the cloud of wasps to disappear enough for me to open the door and drag him in.

I saw it instantly—the chink in his armour. His Achilles' heel. Except it wasn't a heel so much as a wrist. I'd forgotten that Mom had said Sammy needed a new snowsuit. There was about four inches of bare skin between his gloves and sleeves, and I could already see a few red bumps forming. The look on Sammy's face was a mix of pain and anger; I pretended not to notice.

The rest of the day, I went out of my way to be extra nice. In total there were six battle wounds—two on his right wrist, four on his left. Dark red splotches with a white bump in the middle. I knew that if he were still upset when Mom and Dad got home I'd be in trouble, so I brought him ice to put on the stings and told him how brave I thought he was. But it didn't matter. He sat sulking on the couch and nothing I did or said could make him feel better. Finally, I thought of the one way I could always get Sammy to cheer up.

I ran up the creaky wooden steps to the second level of our

house. Sammy and I shared a bedroom at the end of the hall. Our room was small with nothing but a dresser, bunk beds and a night table with an old lamp on it. The lampshade was tilted and broken. Since our room faced east, we always left one of Mom's quilts over the window so the sun didn't wake us too early in the morning.

I ran to the bedside and dropped to my knees. The storage space under the beds was split half-and-half but Sammy didn't really understand what a half was, so my side was bigger.

I pulled out a tin cookie container and opened it up. Inside there was an assortment of crinkled papers and an old, leather-bound journal. I grabbed the journal and raced back downstairs.

Sammy was sitting on the sofa looking through his baseball card binder. I walked up with an air of importance about me, trying to draw attention to the journal beneath my arm.

When he didn't look up, I shut his binder.

"Hey! I'm looking at those!" Sammy said angrily, but when he saw the journal he sat up quickly. "Do I get a Level?"

"I've been going through the details of today's mission over and over again trying to figure out if it warranted a Level. On the one hand, it could be argued that the mission was a complete failure. Many wounds were sustained and I've since looked at the enemy's fortress and little seems to have changed in the way of their numbers." Sammy's smile faded and disappointment flooded his face. "BUT...Levels aren't based only on the success of a mission. Things like valour, bravery, courage, and commitment to the team are also factored in. After long hours of meticulously examining every detail of today's operation, the committee has decided to award you your next Level." Sammy's eyes brightened, his lips started to form a smile but he quickly suppressed it as much as he could; he knew what a serious occasion receiving a Level was.

In the two years since I'd inaugurated the Level system as a method to make my little brother do nearly anything, he had slowly but surely passed through a number of Levels in exchange for the hardships I'd put him through. Ant—his first—was received for sticking his finger in a crayfish's claw to see how much it hurt; Fly was awarded for sneaking down one night to steal food from the fridge because I was hungry, a mission he was caught for but never confessed my involvement; Beetle for retrieving our basketball from deep within Mom's rosebushes; Worm for eating a worm; Snail for mowing the lawn all summer for me, a Level that was revoked when Dad told him he wasn't allowed to do my work, but that was regained for not telling on me when I stuck a stick in the spokes of his bike and made him fall. His last Level, Rabbit, was for lying to Mom and telling her that he had broken the lampshade in our room.

I was already the highest Level possible, Eagle. Of course, I'd never actually done anything to get it. I just made up elaborate stories of walking over lava and fighting dinosaurs and eating scorpions and told Sammy it had all happened before he was born. He believed every word of it. He believed anything I said.

"Sammy, the committee has decided to award you the Level of Fox for the bravery you demonstrated today in Operation Bee Elimination. Of course, like all missions, the information is completely classified."

"What does classified mean?" Sammy asked.

"It means the same thing as Top Secret, you can't tell anyone.

All missions are classified. You didn't know that?"

"Oh...no." Sammy looked disappointed with himself.

"It's a word they say in the army. Only people who actually do the missions can know about them. If you tell anyone something that's classified you get shot." Sammy's eyes went wide. "So yeah, don't tell anyone about our mission."

He thought for a second then agreed.

Later that afternoon, I went back to the journal and opened it. The first page read "Levels—Top Secret" in cursive writing I'd done using the 'Easy Steps to Learning Calligraphy' set Mom had bought me a few years before. Underneath in plain block writing I'd written, "Awarded to members of the team who demonstrate bravery, valour, honour and loyalty to the clan."

All of the other pages contained colourful drawings of animals with a small entry below explaining what the task had been to get that Level.

I flipped to a fresh page and carefully drew a picture of a fox with pencil crayons. It took me over an hour and when I was done it looked sort of like a fox, sort of like a dog. Underneath I wrote, "For bravery demonstrated in Operation Bee Elimination. Calvin Sinclair. July 12, 1995." Then I signed it to make it official.

CHAPTER 3

THE START OF THAT SUMMER CAME AND WENT THE SAME AS THE previous one. Sammy and I spent most of our time exploring the woods behind the house or playing in the creek that ran through it. Dad had built a fort in the low branches of a tree not far into the woods and on rainy days we'd sit inside and read.

I should rephrase that. I read. Sammy listened.

Sammy couldn't read more than "Spot was a dog." He was bad at reading because he never practiced like Mom said he should. Instead he'd just beg and beg and beg until I'd read one of my *Goosebumps* books out loud. I'd only agree because I liked watching him squirm at the scary parts. Before I'd start, I'd always make him promise not to get nightmares. He'd swear he wouldn't, but it didn't matter—he'd still get nightmares. In the evenings after a particularly scary chapter, I'd hear him crawl from his bottom bunk after he thought I was asleep. He'd cross the room to his dresser and fish out the stuffed alligator that he called his 'Elligator' from underneath. It was his comfort toy but he kept it hidden since I'd called him a baby one time during a fight.

"I'm not a baby!" he'd argued.

"Then why do you still sleep with a stuffed animal?"

The next night Elligator was gone.

He didn't even tell Mom where it had gone when she asked—he just shrugged and said he wasn't sure.

Really, I couldn't have cared less if he still had a stuffed animal. I just had a bad habit of saying mean things when I was mad and Sammy had a bad habit of taking them too personally.

On the days we didn't feel like exploring, we'd play basketball in the driveway. I had just finished grade five at Huxbury Elementary and basketball was the favourite game on the playground. Since Huxbury only went to grade six, I had aspirations of being the best kid in the school the next year. My shot was pretty good but since the driveway was uneven gravel, it was difficult to practice dribbling. Dad had promised that the following year I could join a basketball league in London and he'd drive me to all the practices and games.

Sammy was going into grade two and had basketball aspirations of his own. Bump was the popular game for the younger kids and he had hopes of one day winning—a task that would first require him to be able to throw the ball all the way to the rim. At school there were lower nets but at home, we only had a regular-height net. That summer was the first Sammy was finally able to get the ball as high as the rim. Getting it in, however, was a whole other issue.

So that's how the summer started—a boring affair of having no one to play with but my little brother who couldn't quite read and couldn't quite keep up. Still, I would have gladly spent a hundred hours with Sammy for the chance to miss even one Sunday morning.

Sunday mornings meant church and church meant "Sunday Bests"—code for "most-itchy-and-uncomfortable-clothing-known-to-man." The church itself was an old converted barn that they'd gutted and put pews in. It still smelled like the animals that had lived there and the pews were rotted and gave splinters if you slid along them too quickly.

The pastor's name was Reverend Ramos and he had a funny way of talking. Whenever he'd say a word with an 'R' in it, he sounded like a pirate—or at least that's what Sammy and I thought. Mom said it was because he was from Mexico but we preferred our pirate story. Whenever he said something funny, I'd turn to Sammy and repeat it.

"I am R-r-r-reverend R-r-r-amos," I'd say, and Sammy would laugh.

But then Mom would tell us to be quiet and we'd have to sit for the rest of the sermon being bored.

Yep, Sundays were the worst—every Sunday that is, until the Sunday I met Aleta.

It started off like every other Sunday except that it was pouring rain.

"Psst, Sammy, you awake?" I whispered from my top bunk.

"Ugh...what?" he replied.

The grogginess in his voice told me he hadn't been.

"Nothing, just seeing if you were awake. It's raining." I wanted him to be awake because I was awake.

"Oh."

"At least it's raining on a Sunday so we won't be missing a good morning to play outside."

Our conversation ended there as footsteps in the hall told us Dad was coming to wake us up. On Sundays and school days it was always a game to see how long we could stay in bed.

I heard the creaking of the door opening followed by a few seconds of silence where I did my best not to move a muscle. "Boys?"

I heard Dad whisper. Then, after a few more moments of silence, "I've got great news. Church has been cancelled and we're going to go to Disneyland instead."

I knew better than to believe anything Dad said but Sammy was as gullible as a crow.

"Really?" he replied in a shrill cry.

"A-ha, I knew you weren't asleep," Dad laughed.

"That wasn't nice of you, Harold," I heard Mom say from somewhere behind the door.

Dad left the serious side of parenting to Mom. He wrote a humour column for the *London Free Press* and I guess he had trouble living outside that column. Sammy was his biggest fan; I was a close second.

"Good one, Dad," I heard Sammy say laughing from the bunk below as he climbed out of bed.

I continued pretending I was asleep.

"Come on, Cal, I know you're awake up there too, we can't keep God waiting all day." I heard Dad turn and walk out of the room.

"He's not asleep," Sammy said, stepping up onto his bunk so he could peer over the railing into mine. He stuck his hand out and shook my shoulder.

In one swift motion, I shot up in my bunk and caught him with a punch in his upper arm. He cried out and jumped back down to the ground. For a moment he stood looking up at me, rubbing his arm with a defiant look on his face. I could tell he had it in his mind to say something but instead he stuck out his tongue and walked out of the room.

Church started out the same as it did every other Sunday. Reverend Ramos spoke in his funny voice about news from around town—of which there really was none—then droned on and on about something that might as well have been in Latin because nobody was listening.

We had arrived late that day and had had to squeeze into the second-from-last pew. If the sermon hadn't already started, I would have protested when I saw Tom and Joey in the pew in front of us.

Joey took the first pause in the sermon to turn around. "Hey, Pudge," he said, addressing Sammy, "you're looking fatter than usual. Ever think about getting some exercise? I'd let you ride my new bike but you'd probably just break it if you sat on it." He looked up at his older brother for approval.

Joey was Sammy's age and had tormented my brother endlessly in grade one. Sammy was a bit doughy, but I didn't like someone else saying it. Especially not a Riley. They were known for being mean. Probably because their dad was mean.

Sammy didn't reply. He just looked down at his feet.

Now it was Tom's turn. He turned to me and took a less obvious approach to being a jerk. "You been practicing your basketball?" he asked.

It wasn't really a question; Tom was never interested in anyone but himself, so I didn't answer.

"I have," he continued, "Pops paved part of the driveway so we can dribble."

"Yeah. Maybe you can fetch Tom's water bottle when he's thirsty next year," Joey added.

Sammy had been sitting silently trying to ignore their taunts but that was it. He was fine with them picking on him, but as soon as anyone had something to say about me, he was all fists.

"Yeah, right," he bellowed, way too loud for church, "Cal isn't going to be fetching water bottles for anyone. He's already got his Eagle Level. He'll be the best basketballer at the school next year." His big eyes narrowed into tiny slits as he glared at Joey with such hostility that I thought he would lash out and hit him right there in church.

There was a collective shush from a few people and Mom glared down the pew at us. Tom and Joey quickly turned around when their dad looked at them. He was the only person they listened to.

I didn't mind getting in trouble. I was worked up and ready to add my own two cents. And I would have, had something else not caught my eye.

Not something–someone.

Three people had just walked into the church.

Huxbury wasn't a big town and the church community was even smaller. Everyone knew everyone. So when three newcomers turned up late that Sunday, everyone noticed. Even Reverend Ramos paused momentarily and smiled at them.

There were two girls and a man who I guessed right away to be their father. The girls looked eerily alike and were wet from the rain. Their dark hair was tied up in matching green bows and their bangs lay matted to their foreheads. The man was tall with a greying beard and a stern look. He ushered the girls into the empty pew behind us and sat stiffly watching the reverend. The older of the two girls looked like she was already in high school and had a similar serious and unwavering look as her father. The younger girl looked to be about my age and didn't for a second seem interested in the sermon. Instead her eyes danced around the church taking in everything. They stopped momentarily on me and I felt the thumping in my chest pick up.

Gosh, she was pretty.

Her crayon-green eyes stood out against her dark hair and I could see the reflection of the candles around the church in them. I looked away quickly with an awkward realization that I'd been staring.

For the rest of the sermon, I managed to secretly watch her while pretending to pay attention to the reverend. She continued to glance around the church for a while before stopping to grab a hymnbook from the pew in front of her. She thumbed through the pages at a pace that made it obvious she wasn't really reading.

After a while, she lay the hymnbook open in her lap and slowly reached her hand inside her raincoat pocket. As she did so, she wore an expressionless look on her face and stared toward the front of the church. She worked slowly and carefully, withdrawing her hand in slight increments every few seconds so that it was almost unnoticeable. When her hand was finally free from her pocket, it was tightly wrapped around a small paperback.

I recognized the book immediately. I couldn't believe it! It was the latest R.L. Stine—*The Barking Ghost.* She carefully manoeuvered the book into the crease of her open hymnbook and held them both together in such a way that the smaller *Goosebumps* book disappeared inside.

I guess I was pretty caught up staring because I nearly jumped from my seat when I felt Sammy's elbow jab me in the side.

"Oucchhh," I hissed, careful to keep my voice quiet.

"Sorry," Sammy replied. I looked down at him and for a second he looked ready to get up and run, but when he saw I wasn't ready to wallop him, he turned his attention elsewhere. He glanced to where the newcomers were sitting then back to me again.

"Who is she?" he asked.

"I dunno," I said, shrugging my shoulders and pretending not to care.

"Does she go to our school?"

"No. Now shush up or you'll get us in trouble again," I said.

But it was too late. Mom was already leaning forward glaring down the pew at us. Her finger was up to her mouth and her eyes looked like a bull's, ready to charge.

I glared angrily at Sammy and he shrank back into the pew and stopped talking.

Throughout the sermon, I took every chance I had to look back. Each time we were called to sit or stand, I turned around and pretended to be looking around the church, then quickly stole a glance at the newcomer.

She was never looking my way. Her eyes remained trained on the hymnbook in her hands.

Sammy kept nudging me to say something but I pretended not to notice.

Who was she? Where was she from? I had to think of a way to talk to her.

As the sermon came to an end, I rushed to put on my jacket and appeared impatient to get going.

"What's the big hurry, honey?" Mom asked, staring inquisitively at me. "Are you feeling all right?"

"I really have to go to the washroom. Do you think we can hurry and not talk to Reverend Ramos today?"

I knew it was a long shot. Mom and Dad always stayed behind to chat with the reverend. I needed to get out before the girl left so I could think of a way to talk to her.

Mom looked at Dad and he gave a nod.

"When you gotta go, you gotta go," he said.

We started toward the back of the church and I realized my mistake immediately. She was walking toward the front. The aisle was packed with people going this way and that—some to the front, most to the back—and we were caught in the stream like salmon. At the back of the church, I turned for one last glance and as I looked, I saw her head swivel around. Her movement was deliberate. She had just been looking my way.

But had she been looking at me? I wasn't sure.

The only sure thing was it wouldn't take any persuasion to get me to church the next week.

CHAPTER 4

I SAT AT HOME WATCHING THE CLOCK AS THE SECONDS TURNED TO minutes, the minutes to hours, the hours to days—or so it felt. It was only one o'clock. I had been home from church a mere three hours.

"Wanna play Crazy Eights?" Sammy asked, standing in the doorway of the living room, a deck of cards in his hand.

I had been sitting on our old, brown sofa with a *Goosebumps* book closed in my lap staring absently across the backyard to the knee-high corn stalks standing like rows of soldiers beyond. It was still raining and the lawn looked like a giant puddle with hair.

I always thought it was weird: we lived in the country but didn't have a barn, or animals, and the fields all belonged to someone else. We were a small weed among endless stretches of actual farmland—it just didn't make sense.

Still, my parents worked hard to keep our weed as sightly as possible. I think it was a big part of why we moved to the country in the first place—more room to garden. Our whole house was lined with inconveniently placed rosebushes, hard-not-to-step-on daffodils and many more flowers I actively chose not to learn the names of. My parents called themselves hobby gardeners and said it was relaxing. Sammy could sometimes be lured into helping but I had a very different definition of relaxing and pulling weeds wasn't a part of it.

Outside our bedroom window, there were two Japanese cherry trees that in my eyes were the only good part of the garden. When we'd first moved to Huxbury, Dad had joked that there was one for each of Sammy and me—a big one and a small one—and he'd told us to name them. I'd decided on Big Tree, which you can imagine took me all of five seconds to come up with. Sammy had spent days thinking of a name for his tree. In the end, he'd gone with Sakura after Dad told him it was the Japanese word for cherry tree. He was excited to have his own tree and utterly disappointed when we learned the following spring that Sakura was a dud. At the end of April, Big Tree transformed into a radiant ball of white flowers that filled the whole house with a delicious smell while Sakura remained bald and ugly. I suggested to Sammy that maybe it was because he didn't love his tree enough or look after it. Really, it was because Sammy was never lucky with anything.

"Cal? You want to play Crazy Eights?" Sammy repeated.

I'd forgotten that he was still standing in the doorway.

"No. Leave me alone," I said. "I'm reading."

I picked up my book to look occupied.

"Can you read out loud?" he asked, starting to move into the room.

"Not right now. Just go away."

Sammy could be so suffocating. All I wanted to do was sit and think. I had been trying to devise a plan to find out more about the mysterious girl from church and now he was interrupting my thoughts.

He walked slowly across the living room watching me carefully, like I were some rabid dog that might jump up and bite him at any second. When he made it to the chair opposite me he sat down and pretended to look at a magazine from the table beside him. I knew as well as he did that he couldn't read it and every so often I'd catch him casting stupid looks my way as if he wanted to tell me something.

"Aleta Alvarado," he finally said, his secret bursting from inside as he put the magazine down.

"What?"

"The girl at church today. Her name is Aleta Alvarado. And her sister's name is Raquel. They just moved here."

Sometimes Sammy's intuition amazed me. It was like he had a wire straight to my brain and could read my thoughts. How had he known I'd been thinking about her?

"Uh...what...where did you hear that?" I asked.

"Mom told me."

I thought for a moment.

"How did Mom know?"

"Someone in town told her. They moved into Mr. Wilson's old house."

I knew the one he meant. It had been empty since Mr. Wilson died. We didn't know him well but we had gone to his funeral. It was really boring and the only good part would've been to see the dead body but he had been cremated. The house was on Thornton Road, only a fifteen-minute bike ride away.

In the end, I did play cards with Sammy. I thought maybe it would help pass the time as I waited for the rain to stop. I cheated and won, as always, but that never seemed to bother Sammy. He'd grown up losing and by now he was used to it. He just seemed happy enough identifying when he could and couldn't play a card and when he remembered what each meant.

"Two of spades," he'd say. "Pick up two."

I'd put on a look of feigned disappointment, pick up two from the pile, then play the three other twos I'd swiped from the discard pile. "Pick up eight."

"Ah, darn," he'd say, not really disheartened. "Lucky you had those." It never occurred to him that all the twos had been played already and that there was no way I could've gotten them without cheating.

Periodically, I'd look outside to see if the rain had let up, only to find the lawn still covered in ripples. As dusk set in, I forced myself to realize it wasn't in the cards, so to speak, for me to make my way over to Thornton Road that night.

Tomorrow, I thought. Tomorrow I'll go.

During the summer, our bedtime was later and poorly enforced. It was easy to stay up late playing cards or games or whatever else we felt like. That night we were in bed and reading well before our usual time. I read a few chapters out loud from *Say Cheese and Die!* using my best scary-ghost voice at the parts I thought would be most likely to give Sammy nightmares. When Sammy was asleep I lay in bed, eyes closed, listening to his even breathing, wishing I was asleep too. I never was good at falling asleep, especially when I was excited about something.

CHAPTER 5

THE NEXT MORNING I WOKE TO SUN FLOODING THROUGH OUR bedroom window. I'd removed the quilt the night before; I'd wanted an early start on the day.

"Hey, Sammy, you up?"

"Yeah, it's too bright in here. Why'd you take the blanket off the window?"

"It's not a blanket, it's a quilt. And I dunno, thought maybe we could go for a bike ride today."

"Can we go later? Dad said we could make chocolate chip cookies this morning."

Sammy and Dad loved to bake: cookies, muffins, pound cake, tortes, cupcakes—you name it, they made it. I didn't share their sweet tooth. Which was probably why I was skinny and Sammy was, well, chubby.

I glanced at the clock on the dresser—7:25. I was being too anxious. We'd probably ride by her house and she wouldn't even be up yet. I rested my head back on the pillow and stared at the ceiling.

"Yeah, okay, we'll wait a little bit, I guess."

After breakfast, I went out front and shot the ball around while Sammy and Dad made their cookies.

"Three seconds left on the clock, Huxbury is down by one, Calvin Sinclair has the ball. Three...two..." I hurled the ball into the air, flicking my wrist at the end with perfect form. "One...eeeehhh-hhhh!" The ball caressed the nylon of the net and fell on the gravel of the driveway. I'd run through this situation countless times, sometimes ending well, sometimes with the depressing clang of the ball hitting the rim or backboard and bouncing away.

"Yay!" Sammy cheered.

I hadn't noticed him standing in the front doorway of the house.

"Thanks," I said unenthusiastically, trying to make it seem like it was no big deal. "You ready to go?"

"Yeah. Where are we going? Are we riding to meet the new people?"

Again, Sammy's intuition startled me.

"Sure. If you want we could ride that way."

"Yeah, then I can bring them some cookies!"

Perfect! A plan for stopping by and I could say it was Sammy's idea!

Just then, Mom popped through the door behind Sammy. Her hair looked messy as if she had just woken up. "What are you boys up to today?"

"We're going to bring the new people cookies," Sammy chimed.

I groaned inwardly. I'd have preferred to keep the trip to ourselves.

"That's a nice idea," Mom said, rubbing Sammy's shoulders from behind. She paused and looked at something on Sammy's back. "Sammy, where did you get this bruise?" She lifted his sleeve to reveal a huge purple and black mark on the meaty part of his shoulder.

Sammy looked down at his shoulder inquisitively then looked over at me with eyes that asked, "What should I say?" I recalled the punch I'd given him the morning before. Had I hit him that hard?

Sammy pulled down his sleeve and wiggled out from under Mom.

He shrugged his shoulders as if he didn't know where the bruise was from but Mom easily saw through it.

She glared at me.

"Cal?" she asked sternly.

I didn't reply. I knew there was no way out of it.

"You have to stop being so rough with your brother. Look at his arm. He's not a punching bag."

I considered explaining that I had barely hit him but decided it was a waste of breath. "Sorry, Sammy," I said.

We walked to the garage and grabbed our bikes under Mom's continued stare. I could tell she was debating whether or not to continue the lecture, so I jumped on my bike and started riding away quickly.

"Hey! Wait up!" I heard Sammy yell from behind.

The sun was already above the trees and the humid Ontario heat seeped through our clothes. There wasn't so much as a wisp of wind to dull the onslaught.

We turned out of our driveway onto County Road 11 pedalling at an ill-advised pace. Sammy's bike was a lot smaller so he had to pedal twice as hard to keep up. Fifteen minutes later, we were verging on heat stroke as we turned down Thornton Road. My mouth felt like sandpaper and my shirt was drenched with sweat.

"Almost...there..." I heard Sammy gasp from behind as we closed in on Mr. Wilson's old house. His bike swerved left and right as he laboured to push down the pedals.

When we neared the long driveway that led to the Wilson's, I heard a dog barking, distant and nonthreatening at first, but closer with each successive cry. Looking down the driveway, I saw a large black dog barrelling down on us. Immediately all the exhaustion I had just felt dissipated and a wave of adrenaline surged through me. Head down, knuckles white, I pedalled hard and fast past the driveway. I didn't think to turn around until I had gone a hundred metres down the road. Finally—out of breath and lightheaded—I turned around to a horrific sight.

Sammy lay flat on his back with his bike beside him. The dog was on top of him, pouncing at his face while Sammy kicked and flailed to push him back. My mind reeled as I thought of a way to help. Two boys were no match for an angry dog. I looked around for a rock or branch or anything to use as a weapon but there was nothing. All the while, Sammy's screams echoed down the country road. Just before I had made up my mind to pedal back and take my chances with the dog, I heard another voice.

"Chloe, stop! Stop that right now!"

Running down the driveway was the older girl I had seen in church.

"Bad dog, Chloe!" she said, reaching where Sammy lay shrieking on the ground. She grabbed the dog by the collar and pulled it off Sammy.

I pedalled back over and dropped my bike beside Sammy's. He wasn't the gory mess I'd expected. A single stream of blood trickled from his knee down his shin but that was the only sign of injury I could make out on his whole body.

"Are you okay, Sammy?"

He looked shocked and a little upset but he wasn't crying.

"That dog knocked me off my bike and slobbered on me," he said, with a pouting face. "And you just rode away."

He looked on the verge of tears and I felt my face flush as the girl looked at me. Great first impression, I thought.

"I can't even begin to tell you how sorry I am," the girl said as she held back the dog that was still trying to pounce at Sammy as if it were some sort of game. "She has a thing about chasing bicycles but she's completely harmless, I promise."

Sammy seemed satisfied by this and stuck out his hand to let the dog lick him. He giggled and pulled his hand back again, the pouting gone.

"I'm Raquel," the girl said, turning to me, "we just moved here last week." She stuck out her hand and I shook it.

"I'm Cal," I said. "I think we saw you in church."

"Oh, yeah, I thought you two looked familiar."

Her huge smile revealed rows of perfectly straight, white teeth and she had the same green eyes I'd noticed in her sister.

"I'm Cal's brother," Sammy said, holding out his hand. Raquel bent down slightly so she was closer to his height and shook it.

"Yes, I can see that. You two look really alike. What's your name?"

"Sammy," he said, a broad smile crossing his face as he looked over at me. He loved when people said we looked alike. I hated it. We looked nothing alike! Okay, the brown hair and eyes maybe, but I was like a foot taller and not chubby.

"I made you some cookies," Sammy said, turning back to Raquel and holding up his knapsack. He put it on the ground and unzipped the top, but when he looked inside his face showed utter disappointment. He pulled out the Tupperware container but instead of chocolate chip cookies it now appeared to contain a blob of melted, slimy dough.

Raquel picked up on this immediately.

"Oh, thank you, Sammy! I bet if we put them in the fridge they'll be as good as new in no time. It's boiling out here. Why don't you guys come inside and have a drink? I have fresh lemonade."

"Okay!" we agreed.

As we walked down the driveway toward the house, I noticed the curtains in one of the rooms upstairs close quickly—someone had been watching us.

CHAPTER 6

THE INSIDE OF THE HOUSE SHOWED EVIDENCE OF A RECENT ARrival. Unpacked boxes were scattered around the kitchen while piles of wrapping paper lay in the corner. Raquel went about getting Sammy and I lemonade while we sat at the table.

"So where did you guys move from?" I asked.

"We just moved from London," Raquel replied, rooting around in the fridge as she spoke, "Have you guys always lived out here?"

"No, we're from London too. We moved here two years ago so my parents could have a change of scenery," I said, with much more disdain in my voice than I'd meant.

"Yeah? I guess you could say the same about us. We needed a change of scenery."

Raquel placed a tall glass of lemonade with ice in front of each of us, then walked toward the back hall. "Stay here a minute, okay? I'll be right back. I want you guys to meet someone."

I sat drinking my lemonade in silence for a minute, staring at the pulp floating aimlessly in the glass. When I looked up at Sammy I noticed he was doing the same, but not in the anxious way I was—his face had gone back to looking upset. I knew why.

"Jeez, I thought you were a goner back there," I said, trying to force a laugh.

"Yeah..."

Sammy's voice was quiet and he didn't look up from his glass.

"As soon as I saw that dog coming, I didn't even think, I just pedalled as fast as I could."

"Uh huh."

"Oh come on, Sammy, you can't blame me for riding away. I thought you were right behind me."

No reply.

I hated when Sammy was upset. He'd adopted the same guilt trip method Mom used on us when she was mad. No matter what I said or did he would continue to sulk and time was the only Band-Aid.

Raquel walked back into the kitchen. She paused momentarily before speaking, as if what she were about to say required planning. "I wanted you to meet my sister, Aleta, but she's...not feeling too great today so she's going to stay up in her room."

"Maybe she's got the flu," Sammy suggested. "I had it and Mom said I had a feber."

"Fever," I mumbled under my breath.

Raquel gave a thin-lipped smile. "No, she doesn't have the flu. She, well, she's just not feeling herself today."

Sammy seemed to be mulling this over in his head. While he did, Raquel turned to me.

"How old are you, Cal?" she asked.

The question caught me off guard. I felt like an idiot when I had to stop and think before I answered.

"Eleven," I said.

"So you're going into grade six next year?"

"Yep."

"And you go to Huxbury Elementary, right?"

"Yep."

"Do you think you boys can keep something between just the three of us?"

"Sure," we both answered simultaneously.

"I'm a little worried about my sister. She's going to Huxbury Elementary at the end of the summer and she won't know anyone. She hasn't spoken much since...well, for a few months now, and I think it would be really good if she got to know someone before school started, especially someone in her own grade." She looked at me. "She's shy though, so maybe it would be easier if you'd just go up and try to talk to her. Would you mind?"

I shrugged and said I didn't mind.

Raquel led me up a set of blue-carpeted stairs to a hall of doors. She knocked on the first and a quiet voice replied, "Who is it?"

"It's me again. I brought someone who wants to say hi." She gave me a nod toward the door.

There was a long, awkward pause while I stood waiting. Finally, the door creaked open and the same girl I'd seen in church stood looking at the ground in front of me.

"Hi, umm, I'm Cal, I think I might be in your class next year so I just wanted to say hello."

"Hi," she practically whispered back, her eyes still on the floor.

Raquel retreated back down the stairs, leaving the two of us alone.

"Umm, so I hear you are going to Huxbury next year," I repeated. "I thought maybe it would be cool to get to know each other. I only started there last year and, man, I'd wished I'd known someone beforehand. It's not an easy place to fit in, especially being from the city. Most of the kids grew up out here and know each other pretty good. If you wanted to, you know, hang out or whatever, we only live a few kilometres down County Road 11."

She didn't speak but I thought I saw her head nod slightly. At least a few hairs on her head seemed to shake a little. That was enough for me.

"Maybe we could go for a bike ride or something? Do you have a bike?"

Again, only a slight nod, this time a little more obvious.

"I could come by tomorrow morning and meet you. We could bike into town and I could show you the school. It'll be empty and locked, but at least I can show you the playground."

She hung her head lower so that her hair drooped over her face. The only noise in the room was her sock on the carpet as she toed at some invisible object on the ground. We stood for what seemed like an hour. If she had thought that maybe I would leave, she was wrong. I stood waiting for an answer. Had I known back then that it would never come, that Aleta's voice had left her months before, I wouldn't have waited so long.

"Okay, is that a yes?" I finally asked.

Sensing that I wasn't leaving without confirmation, she looked up. Glints of the sun streaming through the window reflected off her eyes and in them I saw something I couldn't quite place. She studied me momentarily, perhaps deciding what my intentions were. Satisfied with what she saw, she nodded and whispered, "Sure," in a voice that was only perceptible because the house was midnight silent.

"Okay, great. I'll come by around nine," I said.

I tried to play it cool but a sheepish grin spread across my face. She closed the door without another word and I felt as light as a dust speck floating through the air as I walked back downstairs.

Sammy and Raquel were chatting away at the kitchen table. He looked happier and his trademark sulk wasn't there anymore.

"How'd it go?" Raquel asked, as I walked into the room.

"Good. We're going to hang out tomorrow."

Her eyes widened and she stared at me, scanning my face for the hint of a joke.

"She said she'd go out tomorrow? That—that's wonderful," she stammered.

It was wonderful. I finally had someone my own age to hang out with. And despite the obvious problem that conversation would be difficult, I was looking forward to a day without constantly explaining things or being relied on. Besides, having someone around who was a little on the quiet side would be a nice change.

"Yep, I'll be by tomorrow at nine for a bike ride."

CHAPTER 7

FIRSTS OF ANYTHING ARE OFTEN EASY TO REMEMBER—LIKE THE first time I went to a movie theatre or my first day of Kindergarten. That first bike ride with Aleta will forever be a part of my memory, but I'll write about it all the same.

I'd hoped to be the first up that morning but I found Sammy's bunk already empty when I climbed down from my own. Teeth brushed, hair wet to flatten the cowlick where I'd slept, I headed downstairs to find Mom, Dad and Sammy sitting around the kitchen table.

"Ah, the young prince has arisen. I hear you have a date today," Dad said, taunting me from behind his morning paper.

"It's not a date," I mumbled, sitting down in the empty chair.

"Harold, stop teasing the kids," Mom scolded.

"Teasing? Who's teasing," Dad said with a smile. "So, what's she like, where's she from, are you going to take her somewhere fancy or low key?"

"It's not a date," I repeated. "We're just going for a bike ride."

"Ah, low key it is. I like your style. I remember the first time I took your mother out. Red Lobster on a Saturday night. Would have been a perfect evening if I'd remembered my wallet."

"It was Oscar Taylor's, and seriously, stop, or he'll never talk to another girl as long as he lives."

"Oscar Taylor's? Really? Huh, Red Lobster must have been with someone else. Hard to keep track of them all." Dad winked at Sammy and me.

Mom rolled her eyes and got up to clear the table.

Sammy had been sitting patiently watching Dad torment me with a grin on his face—he thought Dad was hilarious.

"Mom packed us some snacks for our bike ride," Sammy said, finally having his time to talk.

The night before, as I'd lay in bed imagining my bike ride with Aleta, Sammy had not been in the picture. How could I have been so stupid? Of course Sammy would have assumed he was invited. He was like the leech that got stuck to my foot one time in the creek—impossible to get rid of. The thought crossed my mind to tell him he wasn't allowed to come, but I knew it would only encourage Dad's teasing so I let it go. Maybe having Sammy there for the first time I hung out with Aleta might not be such a bad thing. At least if the conversation went completely dry he'd be there with one of his usual comments about the clouds looking like animals or the cornfields looking beautiful. If anything, he might be good for comic relief.

After a short breakfast, we grabbed our bikes off the lawn where we'd left them and set out on our way. It was another hot, humid day but this time we packed water. I was anxious to get there and had to yell at Sammy more than a few times to stop dawdling. I'd turn around to find him staring off in the distance, bike zigzagging back and forth over the gravel road.

"Hurry up, Sammy! Pay attention to where you're going!"

He'd focus for a few minutes, face determined as he'd push

heavily on his pedals to catch back up, only to forget two minutes later and start dawdling again.

Sometimes he'd yell something from behind but I'd pretend not to hear.

"Dad says it will be a good harvest this year because the corn is already so high," he said. Then, two minutes later, "Cal, what's a harvest?"

I was glad when I heard Chloe barking in the distance. We hopped off our bikes and walked them down the driveway so she wouldn't topple us over. The door was closed so we knocked and waited. Heavy footsteps approached after a few minutes and the door opened to reveal the same man we'd seen in church with Aleta and Raquel.

Up close I could make out grey wisps throughout his beard and he didn't look especially happy to see us. His eyes scanned Sammy and me then he motioned us to come inside without saying a word. We followed him into the kitchen where he pointed at the table.

"Have a seat here." His voice had an accent sort of like Reverend Ramos and he didn't sound very welcoming.

I looked at Sammy and was glad to see he looked every bit as nervous as I felt.

After a moment, we heard voices, low, but distinct, coming from upstairs. I strained my ears to hear but couldn't, so I stood up and walked over to the edge of the kitchen. Sammy waved at me to come back. He looked scared. From my closer spot I could make out the voices and most of what was said.

"I don't like Aleta going out with some boys she only met yesterday," I heard Mr. Alvarado say.

"Aleta needs to get out of the house and do something. You're the one who's always saying that, so why are you suddenly so against her doing it?" The new voice was Raquel's.

"I know, I know, but aren't there any nice girls around here?"

"We don't know anyone here yet and Aleta is eleven, she's old enough to hang out with boys, and that's something you're just going to have to accept, Papa."

"Well, it's fine if you go too."

Raquel let out an exasperated sigh.

"Papa, I'm sixteen years old, Aleta doesn't need a babysitter anymore and besides, I don't have a bike."

There was a long, silent pause, then finally Mr. Alvarado spoke again.

"You come back before dinner, Aleta."

I heard a door slam, then footsteps. They were coming back downstairs so I quickly darted back to the table. Mr. Alvarado entered, looked around, huffed and walked back out.

Man, was I glad Sammy had come. I was shaking all over I was so nervous. I would've felt more welcome in a woman's washroom.

Sammy leaned in close and whispered, "Should we go?"

The idea had definitely crossed my mind. There was a big part of me that wanted to get up and run out of the house but then, there was an even bigger part of me that wanted to stay. I'm not sure exactly what it was but there was something about Aleta that made me want to get to know her—something intriguing. Maybe it was the *Goosebumps* book I'd seen her reading, or maybe it was the thought of having a friend a short bike ride away, or maybe it was that she was so pretty it was hard not to think about her. I dunno, but whatever it was it kept me glued to my seat until we heard footsteps coming down the stairs.

Raquel, followed by Aleta, walked in.

"Sorry to keep you waiting," Raquel said, walking up to the table. Aleta held back a few steps looking at her favourite spot—the floor by her feet. Raquel turned around and grabbed her by the sleeve of her shirt, pulling her over. "Aleta's ready."

After a few warning words from Raquel on riding safely and watching for cars, we were on our way. Raquel held Chloe while we rode down the driveway. I looked back once and saw a dark figure lurking in the upstairs window and felt relieved when we were a few hundred feet down Thornton Road and the house was out of sight.

For the first while we rode in silence, Aleta and I side-by-side in front, Sammy close behind. The air was muggy and hot, the sky a pale blue between scattered clouds and above us two hawks circled, looking for unsuspecting field mice. All in all it was a good day for a bike ride.

"So you used to live in London, huh?" I asked, trying to start up a conversation.

I think maybe Aleta didn't hear me over the sound of rushing air or else she had nodded and I'd not seen.

I tried again.

"We used to live in London too. What school did you go to?"

"Ryerson," she replied without elaboration. This time I heard her clearly.

"Oh yeah, that's downtown right? We went to Blythewood. Well, I did, Sammy wasn't in school yet."

I turned around to see if Sammy had heard this only to find that he had already fallen way behind.

"Hurry up, Sammy!" I yelled.

Aleta looked behind too and we both slowed to let Sammy catch up. When he got close, I noticed he was already out of breath. It was unusual—Sammy was chubby, sure, but he wasn't usually that slow.

"You're riding like a turtle with four broken legs," I joked, then stole a look at Aleta to see if she had smiled.

She hadn't. Instead she looked concerned.

I was kind of annoyed that Sammy was already slowing us down. "Come on, Sammy, we can stop for water when we're halfway."

As we continued riding, I tried again to get Aleta to talk.

"So were you on any teams at Ryerson?" I asked.

"Cross-country," she replied.

"Oh, so you like to run?"

She nodded.

I waited for her to ask me what sports I played so I could tell her how good at basketball I was but she didn't say anything. I realized I wasn't getting anywhere asking questions so I started just talking.

"I think you'll like Huxbury. I mean, the school itself isn't much—it's pretty small and all the classrooms are in portables—but the teachers and most of the kids are nice. The only ones you've gotta watch out for are Tom and Joey. You probably saw them in church—the two boys with really short, black hair? They sit with their dad who always looks angry?"

I looked at Aleta but she made no sign that she knew who I was talking about. She was still staring straight ahead but I could tell she was listening.

"I'll point them out next Sunday. They're the meanest kids in Huxbury and maybe even the meanest kids on the face of the earth. Tom will be in our class. Don't worry though—you'll learn to ignore him. Plus, I'll be there to make sure he doesn't bother you."

Aleta smiled at this. It flashed quickly and then was gone, but it was definitely a smile.

From then on, things seemed a little bit lighter. We were still a few kilometres from Huxbury but Aleta didn't look so nervous or angry or whatever it was anymore. She stopped staring rigidly ahead and started looking around over the cornfields with a sort of half-smile on her face. She reminded me of Sammy when he was in church trying not to laugh. Her lips were still tight but her eyes had little crinkles beside them that told me she was in a happy place.

Even I was beginning to appreciate the countryside. Sure we were surrounded by nothingness, but right then that nothingness meant we could ride down the middle of the road without having to worry about getting hit by a car or a truck. If we'd still lived in London, there's no way we'd have been allowed to ride down the middle of the road.

We were about halfway to the school when we were torn from our peaceful daydreaming by the harsh sound of metal on gravel.

I turned around to find Sammy buckled over on the side of the road, his legs still wrapped around his bike that now lay on its side, wheels spinning in the air.

"What happened, Sammy?" I yelled, jumping off my bike and running back to where he lay.

When I first looked at him, his eyes had a vacant stare but then he blinked a few times and seemed to come around. He looked up at me with the confusion of someone who'd just fallen asleep on the couch. "What...what happened..." he whimpered.

"That's what I just asked you," I said.

Aleta bent down beside him. "You don't look very well," she said. "Maybe we should take a break and rest." She reached out and touched him softly on the forehead. "You feel really hot."

It was the first time I'd heard Aleta say more than two words strung together. Her voice was sing-songy, pretty with only a slight accent.

"Yeah, let's take a break," I agreed.

We pulled our bikes under a small maple at the side of the road and sat down to cool off. I didn't say it, but I was worried—Sammy really didn't look good. He was dusty white and beads of sweat were pouring down his face. I pulled out the water bottle he had packed in his knapsack and handed it to him.

"You feeling any better?" I asked.

"A...little...bit..." he said, words coming out between short gasps. He was still really out of breath and I was almost sure he wouldn't be able to make it the rest of the way into Huxbury.

I looked around for a house to call Mom but we hadn't passed a house in ages. All around us was just corn and more corn.

"We could probably make it into town," I suggested, "it's not that much further. Then we could call Mom and have her pick up Sammy."

Aleta shook her head. "I think we should turn around."

"I'm okay," Sammy said, trying to stand up but looking wobbly.

Aleta was right—we needed to turn around.

"Yeah, okay, we'll turn around."

We pulled Sammy's bike into the first row of the cornfield and lay it on its side so no one could see it from the road, then Aleta helped Sammy up onto my handlebars.

"You sure you're okay with this?" she asked skeptically.

"Yeah, we used to do this all the time before Sammy got rid of his training wheels."

It was the truth but when Sammy used to ride sitting on my handlebars, he was way lighter and way less groggy. It was a really slow, shaky ride home but I managed to get Sammy all the way back without falling.

I helped him into the kitchen and he practically sank into one of the kitchen chairs.

"Mom!" I yelled.

Mom came downstairs with a towel wrapped around her head—she'd evidently been in the shower.

"What's wrong?" she asked, then she saw Sammy slumped over the table.

Mom may have been the stricter parent but when one of us was hurt or sick or sad, she was also the quickest with a hug. She asked what had happened and I explained in detail, or as much detail as I could, about how one moment we were riding our bikes and the next Sammy was lying in the dirt.

"Probably the heat," she offered.

"Yeah, probably," I agreed.

She looked him over for injuries and found only the dark bruises on his shoulder and now, a new set of bruises down his leg.

"Are these from today?" she asked.

Sammy wasn't talking so I answered for him. "No, I think those are from yesterday. He cut his knee when he fell off his bike. That's two falls in two days—maybe we need to put his training wheels back on."

I looked back at Aleta who was still standing by the door to see if she'd found this funny but her eyes had a glassy appearance and she was staring intently at Mom and Sammy.

"You must be Aleta," Mom said, looking across the room while she rubbed Sammy's back. "I hear you and your family just moved to Huxbury. It's nice to meet you."

Aleta didn't say anything. Instead she stood completely still. She seemed hypnotized by the slow, circular motion of Mom's hand on Sammy's back. There was a really awkward silence that seemed to last forever.

"I hear you have a sister," Mom said, trying again.

Again Aleta said nothing.

I felt my ears growing hot. I felt embarrassed. I took a step toward Aleta and that seemed to snap her out of her daze.

"Aleta?" I said, trying to urge her to speak.

Her eyes looked frantically from me then back to Mom again. She looked like she wanted to say something but then thought better of it. Her mouth moved to form words but nothing came out. She stepped backwards, fumbled for the door handle, then turned and ran out.

Without saying a word—just like that—she left.

CHAPTER 8

By the time I had run out the door after Aleta, she was at her bike, picking it off the ground. The once white clouds were now dark and grey and ominous.

"Hey, wait up!" I yelled, jogging up to where the bikes were. "Is everything all right?"

I knew the answer as soon as I saw her. Her green eyes were bigger than ever and tears were streaming down her cheeks.

She looked away.

"Everything is fine," she sniffed, wiping her cheeks with her sleeve. "I just need to get home before my dad starts to worry." Her bad excuse became worse when her voice broke down at the final few words, but before I could offer any comfort she was off, pedalling hard down the driveway toward the road.

"Hey! Hang on, I'm coming with you!" I shouted, grabbing my bike off the ground nearby. "It's going to start to rain soon. Maybe we should wait for my dad to get home so he can drive us."

Whether she was too far ahead to hear or just didn't care to answer, she rode on, not acknowledging me.

I pedalled hard to catch up but she must have been pedalling hard too because we were a good ways down the road by the time I caught her. A light drizzle had started and I knew from the humidity in the air that it would only be a few minutes before that drizzle turned into a torrential downpour.

"Aleta, I really think we should turn back, it's going to start to rain really hard soon."

She looked defiant–like it would take a hurricane to make her turn around. We carried on in silence and as I'd suspected, the rain picked up with every minute. The road became wet and slippery, and the visibility rapidly worsened.

I saw a thick grove of trees ahead. "Aleta..." There was no need to finish; she was already veering off the side of the road toward it. The rain was coming down like a waterfall and I could hardly see her though she was only a few metres in front of me.

We dropped our bikes and ran into the woods, clothes sticking to our bodies like paint.

The trees offered good shelter so the ground was still dry. Aleta sat down, eyes red, hair matted like the first time I'd seen her in church. She was crying still, and the only noises in the forest were the rain hitting the canopy and her soft whimpers.

For a moment I just stood there watching her, unsure why she was crying, unsure what to do about it. But then I thought about Mom and what she did when Sammy or I were sad so I sat down next to her and wrapped my arms around her. I thought she might pull away–I'd only met her two days before–but she didn't. Instead she moved closer into my arms and rested her head on my shoulder, and that's when she broke down. Her quiet whimpers turned to loud sobs and her tears began to flow. I held her tight, not saying a word.

I don't know exactly how long we sat there, I was lost in my own thoughts, but my daze broke when I realized Aleta had stopped crying. I let her go and she slid from my arms and sat back.

"Sorry," she said. Then, more to herself, she whispered, "I promised myself I wouldn't have a sad day."

"A sad day?" I asked.

For a moment she sat chewing her bottom lip and though she was beside me, I could tell her mind was somewhere else. Judging by the way her nose crinkled and her eyebrows turned in—she didn't like where she was. The sleeves of her shirt were wet and bunched up around her elbows and I noticed rows of faint lines running down her forearms. I reached out and touched one of the lines and that seemed to snap her back to the present. She pulled her arm away and rolled down her sleeve.

"Never mind," she said quickly. "We should probably get going. The rain has stopped and I don't want my father to worry." She stood up and walked to the edge of the grove with an urgent look on her face. I wanted to ask her again why she was crying but I knew she didn't want to talk about it, so I stood up and followed.

As we rode silently back toward her house, the clouds cleared and the sun came back out. It was weird, one moment it was raining like we were going to need an ark and the next the sky was blue and clear as if it had never rained at all. The only evidence was the puddles pockmarking the road and we zigzagged to avoid them.

When we got to the end of Aleta's driveway I stopped my bike. I looked at the upstairs window expecting to see a shadow watching but there was no one. Still, I didn't want to go near the house. "I should probably just say goodbye here."

Aleta glanced at her house then back to me.

She grinned and nodded.

I expected her to ride away and that to be the end of that. I figured after the disaster of a day there wouldn't be any more bike rides but to my surprise she stood there looking at me as if waiting for me to say something.

Finally, I broke the silence. "I'm sorry you didn't get to see the school and that Sammy kind of ruined our bike ride and that you... well...that you were feeling sad or whatever. I guess this whole day turned out to be a trainwreck."

"No," Aleta said, shaking her head, "it was fun."

"Fun?"

She nodded. "Yeah, I haven't been out in a while. It was nice."

"Then maybe we could hang out again? We could go for a run or something—you said you liked cross-country. I'm not sure if you noticed but there happens to be a lot of country to cross out here."

I gestured toward the fields around us, and Aleta smiled.

"Sure, we could go for a run."

A part of me had hoped she'd say no and suggest something else. I only suggested the running idea because she'd said she liked cross-country. When we'd done cross-country at school in London, I'd hated it. I was not a long distance runner by any means but if it meant I'd get to spend more time with Aleta—I could suck it up.

I made Aleta repeat her phone number a few times, memorized it, and promised I'd call her soon to figure out a plan. As I turned to ride home Aleta said, "Tell Sammy I hope he's feeling better."

And that's when I realized I'd completely forgotten about my brother.

CHAPTER 9

When I got home, Mom said that Sammy still wasn't feeling well and had already gone to bed. Later that night when I climbed into my top bunk, I could tell he was awake. I could always tell when he was awake by his breathing.

After a few minutes I heard his voice from below.

"Cal? Are you awake?"

"Yeah," I said.

I waited for him to say something but he didn't. Instead the room went back to silence and I realized he hadn't wanted to talk, only to check if I was awake.

"How are you feeling?" I asked.

I felt him shift again in his bunk.

"Hot," he replied.

The room was a little warm—it was summer and we didn't have air conditioning—but it wasn't much hotter than usual.

"Want me to grab you the fan?" I asked.

"No, I'm okay."

I closed my eyes and tried to fall asleep again. I'd put the quilt back over the window so it was pitch black. I was nearly asleep when Sammy's voice woke me again.

"Cal, do you think Elligators live in the river?"

"Sammy, I was almost asleep," I groaned. The room went quiet and I could tell Sammy thought I was mad. "What river?" I mumbled.

"The one by the house."

"You mean the creek in the woods?"

"Yeah."

Normally I would've said yes. I liked teasing Sammy. It was so easy because he believed everything I said but he'd had a rough day and I was feeling nice. "Nah, I'm pretty sure they only live in Africa."

"Oh." He sounded disappointed rather than reassured.

I smiled.

To Sammy, alligators were made of soft plush and were cuddly. There was so much he didn't know. During the day all his questions annoyed me—like I was supposed to be some sort of grade one teacher—but at night, when we'd lay awake talking, I didn't mind so much. I kind of liked that he was still a baby. I kind of liked that he didn't know anything.

"Night, Sammy," I said, rolling over and facing the wall.

"Night, Cal."

It was Thursday morning and the house was empty. Dad had left for London to meet with someone from work and Mom had taken Sammy to the doctor. After two days of barely getting out of bed, headaches and a thermometer that said fever, Mom was suspicious that Sammy had the flu. I'd have been dragged along for the trip had it not been the morning I'd planned to meet Aleta for our run. I'd argued and argued until Mom had given in and said I could stay.

T-shirt, shorts, basketball shoes—I was ready for what I thought would be an easy jog. Over a brief phone call earlier that morning, Aleta and I had decided to run toward each other's houses through the corn fields. We figured we'd eventually cross paths and spot each other but after fifteen minutes of sluggish jogging, I realized it might not be so easy. The corn was waist-high and the fields were infinite. Visions of dying from heat exhaustion in some remote field began to cross my mind when I finally spotted Aleta a few fields over in a bright orange shirt.

As she approached, she looked light and fresh—like she'd only just started running. It was the exact opposite of how I felt but I put on a smile and tried to look as perky as she did.

"Not a bad day for a run," I said, jogging up to her and trying not to gasp for air.

Aleta's hair was tied back with an orange headband that matched her shirt and she was wearing black shorts and white running shoes. To this day I have no idea how they managed to stay so white.

We briefly stood side-by-side looking around, surveying the land, picking a path. Really, it didn't matter, it was all the same—corn to the left, corn to the right. If we were lucky we might get to run past a field of soy. Whoopee!

"Which way?" she asked.

"You lead. I'll follow."

Aleta took off in the opposite direction of our houses, charting an indeterminate course between the fields. I followed closely behind secretly wishing we could slow the pace. If the run had been a game of who could accidentally step in the most mud puddles and boggy spots, I would have won, and soon my heavy basketball shoes grew even heavier. The sun seemed to grow hotter with every passing minute and the tall grass cut at my calves. As the houses shrunk further and further behind us, I thought about how we would have to run further and further back. I desperately didn't want to be the one to call it quits but after what felt like hours (though, quite possibly was only ten minutes) I was ready to throw in the towel. I'd had enough. If I kept going I would pass out just like Sammy had and that—I told myself—was way more embarrassing than asking for a break.

Just as I went to open my mouth and sound my defeat, Aleta yelled, "Why don't we stop in those trees ahead?"

I looked up to find a wall of trees had materialized ahead of us. I hadn't noticed because I'd been staring at my feet. I couldn't believe the fields actually had an end! It was further away than I would have liked but at least I now had something tangible to run toward.

I told myself I could make it.

And I did. Barely.

As soon as I ran into the forest, I collapsed onto the ground. It was soft and dry and the relief from the sun was amazing. I lay there listening to my own breathing and feeling my chest move up and down, up and down. I closed my eyes and felt the cool stillness all around me.

After a while, the quietness began to unnerve me. Where had Aleta gone? I sat up and looked around.

"Aleta?"

She didn't answer so I stood up and walked further into the trees.

"Aleta?"

The forest had looked dense from far away but twenty steps in and I was already coming out the other side. Only it wasn't like I was on the other side of the same forest, it was like I had walked out of a completely new forest. Like it was some sort of gateway to another world.

I found Aleta standing with her back to me, looking out over the landscape. In front of her was a clear pond as smooth as glass and rimmed with bull rushes. White flowers on lily pads dotted the edges and the reflection of the sky in the middle was as clear as the one above. Beyond the pond was a hill so steep it gave the impression that a part of the world had broken off and fallen a hundred feet. I could see all the way to the horizon miles and miles away—it felt like I could see forever.

Only I couldn't look at forever for very long.

Lake Huron was lit by a glaring July sun in the distance and it glistened a brilliant gold and blue—like someone had melted the sky, poured it into a pot of gold then added a million stars. It was like looking into the world's brightest disco ball.

Between the pond and Lake Huron was a landscape of rolling hills and untouched fields; of wild flowers and brambles and dancing long grass. There was no sign of human life—no roads, no houses, no tractors—just a hidden expanse of undiscovered country.

Another world.

I'd never developed Sammy's love for the countryside. I'd never appreciated what Mom and Dad saw in cornfields and dirt roads, but this—this was different. This was a picture taken from a magazine and stretched out in front of me.

"It's beautiful," Aleta whispered beside me.

"Yeah," I said, "it's something."

I walked over to the pond and put my toe into the water, watching as the mud melted off my shoe. Seeping in, the cool water felt like heaven. I put my whole foot in, then the next. I waded into the pond until it was deep enough to swim. The water washed away the sweat and grime. I felt revitalized.

"Aleta, you have to come in. This is amazing."

Aleta hesitated a moment, watching me swim as she appeared to make up her mind. Then she sat down and began pulling off her shoes and socks.

"Leave them on," I said.

"These are new," she replied, then stood and walked to the edge. "And besides, I want to feel the mud squish between my toes."

As she stepped into the pond her eyes closed and her body seemed to melt into the water. She lay along the surface not moving a muscle, yet somehow managing to stay afloat, like driftwood.

On the far side of the pond, I found a trickle of water running down the sloping hill that had made a path of mud. The hill was steep enough that with a running start I could slide all the way down, finishing in a giant heap of muck at the bottom. I convinced Aleta to try it and we spent the rest of the morning sliding down the hill then running back up to wash off in the pond.

When we tired of sliding, we lay beneath the shade of the maple trees and counted the clouds floating by, feeling the warm breeze of summer and listening to the drone of dragonflies amid a chorus of bullfrogs.

I had nearly drifted off to sleep when I heard Aleta whisper, "This place is perfect."

I rolled over to find her sitting up, staring off into the distance. Pieces of dry grass were stuck in her hair and her shirt was dirty from the mud. I guess the pond hadn't completely cleaned us off.

I pulled a piece of long grass from the ground and stuck it in my mouth then lay with my hands behind my head. "I feel like a farmer taking a break after a long morning of hard work."

"Hard work?" Aleta laughed. "Trust me, you don't look like any farmer I know. All we've done is swim and play. I'd say you look more like Huck Finn."

"Who's Huck Finn?"

"Have you never read Mark Twain?" she asked, one eyebrow raised.

"Who's that?"

"He's an author."

"If his name's not R.L. Stine and his books don't say *Goosebumps* on the cover, I'm not interested," I said. "And don't pretend like you don't like *Goosebumps* because I saw you reading one in church the other day." Aleta's face turned red and I grinned. "You're not as sneaky as you think."

She grinned back. "But I'm pretty sneaky."

I laughed. "Yeah, pretty sneaky."

We sat for a little while longer before Aleta said she should probably get home to help her sister make dinner. We walked as far as an old tree trunk that was split and charred in the middle—I guess when you're the only tree between miles and miles of fields your chances of getting struck by lightning are pretty good.

"This is probably midway between our houses," Aleta suggested.

"Yeah, probably," I agreed, feeling suddenly sad that the day was coming to an end.

I didn't want the day to be over. It had been the most fun I'd had since moving to Huxbury. My mind fumbled for a way to ask her to hang out again but asking felt awkward, I needed a reason. Another run? Heck, even that pain was worth it. But then an idea came to my mind and I blurted it out before I had time to think it through.

"We should make the pond our Secret Spot," I said. "We could meet back here tomorrow morning—bring snacks and *Goosebumps* books—then spend the day reading by the pond."

"A Secret Spot?"

"Yeah, you know, a place that only the two of us know about. A safe place we could run away to if Huxbury were ever taken over by pirates or escaped convicts or zombies. I'm pretty sure even the farmers who own these fields don't know about the pond. It'll be a place all to ourselves."

I realized halfway through my speech that I was talking to Aleta as if she were Sammy. The pirates, the escaped convicts, the zombies—these were all stories Sammy and I talked about. We had been searching for a Secret Spot for years. We'd had a few—the creek, a hidden nook behind a bush at the back of the house, the closet in our old home in London—but none of those were actually secret. Mom and Dad always knew about them. The pond was different. It was actually a secret. It was perfect.

Aleta smiled. "I don't think it would be the first place I'd run away to if the town were taken over by zombies but okay, I like the idea, we can have a Secret Spot."

Later that night, Sammy asked me what I'd done all day. It was harder than I thought to keep the secret. A big part of me wanted to say, "We found a pond on the top of a mountain with a mudslide over a thousand feet long and a view so far that if you look at it for too long you go permanently blind."

But a Secret Spot is a secret and I wasn't about to ruin it.

"Nothing," I told him, "just went for a run."

And the Secret Spot remained a secret.

CHAPTER 10

THE FLOOR FELT COOL UNDER MY FEET AS I KNELT AND BEGAN rummaging through the snack cupboard in our kitchen. It was early—really early—and outside it was still pitch black. My parents wouldn't be up for a few hours and I wanted to keep it that way so I was trying to be really quiet. I reached carefully into a box of granola bars, pulled out a handful and put them into my open backpack. The rest of the boxes I tried were empty—I'd been taking snacks all week to the Secret Spot with Aleta so we were running low.

Next I moved to the refrigerator. There wasn't much there either. I'd eaten all the sandwich meats and Mom hadn't gone shopping to replace them yet. I grabbed a couple yogurts and thought about whether they would go bad before we had the chance to eat them. If the weather was as hot as it had been the last few days, they wouldn't last more than a few hours.

I shoved them in anyway.

We could eat them as a mid-morning snack.

I tried to look through my backpack to see what I had so far but it was too dark to see—I hadn't turned any of the lights on for fear of waking someone. I used my hand as my eyes and felt inside the backpack.

Goosebumps book, three bananas, two juice boxes, granola bars and two yogurts—I was all set.

I turned around to leave but let out a sharp cry when I saw someone standing in the shadows behind me.

I cursed myself when I saw that it was only Sammy in his Spiderman pajamas. I hoped I hadn't woken up my parents.

"Jeez, Sammy," I hissed, "don't sneak up on me like that! How long have you been behind me?"

The small silhouette shrugged.

"Why are you up? You should still be asleep—it's really early."

Sammy ignored my question. "Where are you going?" he asked.

"I'm going to meet Aleta," I said. "I have to leave or I'll be late." I started moving toward the door but Sammy followed right beside me.

"But it's still night out."

"It won't be soon and we want to see the sunrise. Which is why I have to go now." I sat down and started pulling on my shoes.

"Can I come?" Sammy asked, sitting down beside me and grabbing his boots.

I let out a long exasperated sigh. "No, Sammy, you can't come. You've had fevers all week. Mom wouldn't be happy if you went outside this early when you're not feeling well."

It was the truth. Sammy had been sick all week. Every morning when I'd gotten up he'd still been in bed—which was not like Sammy to sleep in—and his sheets were always drenched with sweat from his fevers.

Of course there was a bigger reason Sammy couldn't come but I didn't want to mention the Secret Spot or he'd start asking questions.

"But I feel better!" Sammy whined, his voice louder as he sensed I wasn't going to let him come. I knew if I didn't think of something quickly the tears would start and Mom and Dad would wake up.

As usual, my mind went to the Levels.

"Why didn't you say you felt better?" I said, sounding as excited as possible without raising my voice. "I've been waiting for you to get better all week so you could start your daily missions!"

"Daily missions?" Sammy asked, looking confused.

"Tell me you know what the daily missions are?"

Sammy shook his head.

"Oh, all right, I'll explain it. Sometimes I think you don't even care about the Levels. You certainly don't know much about getting them."

"I do care about the Levels!" Sammy said. "I want to be an Eagle!"

"Well, if you want to be an Eagle you better start doing your daily missions. Now that you're feeling better, I'm going to start giving you a mission each day, and if you complete it, you get a Level. Of course the missions are hard work and they'll take you all day—so you won't be able to come with me."

Sammy stopped pulling on his boots and thought this through. "But can't I do it tomorrow? I want to come see the sun."

"No," I said, shaking my head and standing up. I needed to leave and was getting impatient. I was going to miss the sunrise. "It has to start today. Either you decide now or you won't be an Eagle."

Sammy could tell I was serious. "Fine," he said, "I'll do the missions. What do I have to do?"

"Hmm," I said, frantically looking around, trying to think of something quickly—something that would occupy Sammy for the whole day.

I walked over to the sink and opened the cupboard below. Mom kept empty mason jars for making jam and I grabbed one.

"Today's mission is to catch one hundred live ants in this jar."

"One hundred!" Sammy cried.

"Shhhhh! You're going to wake Mom and Dad! Yes, one hundred."

"But I can't do that!"

"Yes you can—I did it to get my Cheetah Level when I was only four. And besides, are you telling me you want to quit before you've even tried? Because I can always find someone else to train—someone who's actually willing to put in the work to become an Eagle."

"No, I do, I do. I mean I will." I passed Sammy the jar and he took it. "It's just that—"

Sammy didn't get to finish his sentence because I was already out the door. I saw him standing on the other side with the jar held tightly to his chest. I felt sorry leaving him behind but it was already starting to get lighter outside and I didn't have time for feeling sorry. I took off running through the backyard at a full sprint.

It was Aleta who had suggested getting up early for the sunrise. We had come back to the Secret Spot every day after discovering it and had spent hours reading beneath the trees. It turned out Aleta liked *Goosebumps* books just as much as Sammy and I. She had read the whole series once and was working on them a second time while she waited for new ones to come out. I hadn't even finished them once—partly because I was a slow reader, partly because Sammy asked so many questions.

But the odd thing about Aleta and her reading was this: every time I looked up at her to see how much further she'd made it through her book, she didn't actually seem to be reading. She spent more time looking out over Lake Huron than actually reading. And all the while she had this look on her face like she was thinking really, really hard about something. Like there was something confusing about the water.

"If you stare at that lake for too long you'll go blind," I finally joked.

Aleta hadn't responded. She just kept staring off into the distance like she hadn't heard me.

"You sure like the view, huh?" I said, trying again to get some sort of response.

"Yeah," she said, still staring at the water.

I went back to reading. When Aleta gave a one-word answer that meant she didn't feel like talking, and when she didn't feel like talking, there was no point trying to force the issue. All I'd get were more one-word answers.

But then to my surprise, she continued, "It reminds me of my auntie's house in Mexico. Of course this is a lake and that was the ocean, but the sun reflects off the waves the same." She was sitting with her arms stretched out behind her and kept looking at the water as she spoke. "My parents used to wake Raquel and me up early on clear mornings and we'd drive down to the beach and sit on a blanket; waiting for the sun. And when it came, the beach changed into the most magical place on earth. The whole ocean would turn orange and gold—the sand, the boats floating offshore—everything, golden. But it would only last a few minutes before it was over. The magic would leave our beach and move on to the next. My mother used to say that people who don't believe in magic don't get up before the sun." Aleta looked at me. "Have you ever seen a sunrise over water?"

I shook my head.

"I bet the sunrise here would be amazing. We should come really early one morning and see."

I liked that idea a lot.

"How about tomorrow?" I suggested.

Aleta hesitated. "Tomorrow? Tomorrow might not..."—she paused, debated it momentarily—"okay, tomorrow. We'll have to be up really early though."

And that's how I found myself running through cornfields at a ridiculous hour. I'd grabbed a flashlight but it wasn't much help. It only gave me enough time to see what I was going to step in—not enough time to avoid it. Still, I ran the entire way without stopping—partly because I didn't want to miss the sunrise, partly because I was scared that if I stopped something would jump out of the corn and eat me.

When I got to the pond it was empty.

"Aleta?"

"Up here," a voice called back. I shined my light up into a maple and found Aleta sitting on a low branch.

"What are you doing up there?"

"Avoiding coyotes," she replied.

I looked around nervously. "You saw a coyote?"

"No, but I thought I heard one. Turns out it was just you. Why are you so late?"

I walked over to the trunk and put my flashlight between my teeth.

"Lung stury," I said. I took the flashlight out of my mouth when I'd settled on the branch next to her. It was a perfect climbing tree with a long horizontal branch for sitting. "Sammy was awake and he wanted to know where I was going."

"Oh," Aleta said, "did he want to come?"

"Nah," I lied. "He was really tired. He was just mad that I woke him."

"Oh, okay. You guys are pretty close, huh?"

"Me and Sammy? Yeah, we're close. I mean, he can be pretty annoying sometimes but then other times he says things that crack me up. Like a couple days ago when he was asking if alligators lived in the river behind our house."

Aleta laughed. "But that's what older siblings are for—answering annoying questions. I used to ask Raquel all kinds of things. We used to be so close before..."

Aleta trailed off. The horizon was starting to change but I felt like that's not why she had stopped talking. There was something about her sister that she didn't want to talk about. She still hadn't told me what made her sad but I could tell she was thinking about it.

"Before what?" I asked.

"Nothing," Aleta said. "The sun is starting to come up. Watch."

I sat quietly watching the water change just as Aleta had described. For a few minutes our Secret Spot became encased in gold.

After the sun was well above the horizon and the morning had officially arrived, Aleta jumped down from the tree.

"I better get going," she said.

"Going?" I exclaimed.

"I can't stay today. We're going to London. It's Friday."

"What happens on Fridays?"

Aleta hesitated. "I get to visit my mother."

"Your mother? She's still in London?"

Aleta nodded.

"Why?"

It was obvious Aleta didn't like the question. "I really need to go," she said, grabbing her flashlight from beneath the tree. "See you tomorrow."

She took one quick glance over her shoulder at the lake, and took off running through the trees.

CHAPTER 11

When I finally made my way back to the house I saw Sammy crouched over the driveway with his face a few inches from the gravel. He was concentrating really hard on what he was doing and didn't notice me coming up behind him so I stopped and watched.

He was trying to cup something into his hands from the driveway but each time he opened them he let out a frustrated groan. He tried again and this time when he opened his hands he seemed momentarily excited. But then he looked closer, his hand only an inch from his nose, and whatever he saw was obviously a disappointment.

"I'm sorry, little guy," he said, using his other hand to pick something off his open palm and putting it on the gravel, "I didn't mean to squish you."

I laughed and Sammy spun around. He smiled when he saw me.

"How's the daily mission going?" I asked, walking up to him.

His smile disappeared and he looked beside him at the mason jar.

"Not very good," he said, hanging his head. "I keep squishing the ants."

"All of them?" I tried not to laugh again. I could tell Sammy was really disappointed.

"Not all of them."

"How many have you caught?"

He grabbed the jar and passed it to me. Inside I saw three ants crawling around. Well, two crawling, one hobbling.

"Three?"

"I had more," Sammy said, his voice sounding upset, "but I put the jar down and it tipped and I didn't see and,"—his voice broke a little—"and they ran away."

I handed him the jar back and ruffled his hair. "That's okay, you'll do better with tomorrow's daily mission, don't worry."

That seemed to make him feel a little better.

"Want to shoot some hoops?" I asked.

"Okay!"

That seemed to make him feel a lot better.

We spent an hour playing basketball before Sammy said he felt tired and went inside for a nap. I kept shooting, all the while thinking about Aleta, the Secret Spot and why her mother still lived in London.

THE NEXT MORNING, before I left for the Secret Spot, I gave Sammy his second daily mission.

"You have to sink one hundred baskets."

I thought Sammy would protest and I was ready to drop it to fifty to be nice but he didn't. Instead he said, "Well, I did make two yesterday!"

"Yep, that's true, and you'll have the whole day today."

I waited for Aleta by the burnt tree for an hour before I decided I must have missed her—she was usually the one waiting for me—so I walked to the Secret Spot by myself. When I got there, I found it vacant except for two ducks swimming in the middle of the pond. I searched around but there was no sign of Aleta.

Had she slept in? Was she running late for some reason? I decided to wait and see if she showed up. The sky was overcast but it was still hot so I went for a swim. I read. I watched Lake Huron.

And still, Aleta didn't show up.

By lunchtime, I convinced myself that she wasn't coming.

As I walked back to the house I thought about what could have happened. Maybe she was sick? But she'd seemed fine the day before. Maybe she'd spent the weekend with her mom? But then why had she said, "see you tomorrow"?

Sammy was playing basketball with Dad when I got home.

"I do have another son!" Dad exclaimed as I walked through the backyard toward them. "I'd completely forgotten!"

"And I'd forgotten how funny you were," I said.

"Want to play?" Sammy asked. "Dad says I'm getting a lot better."

"Fourteen baskets so far today," Dad said. "He seems really intent on getting to one hundred for some reason." Dad eyed me suspiciously and I knew Sammy probably hadn't directly told him about the daily mission, but it was never hard to figure out what Sammy was up to.

"Seems like a good goal," I said, deflecting Dad's suspicious glare and continuing inside. I really wasn't in the mood to play. I wanted to call Aleta's house and find out why she hadn't shown up.

I tried calling twice but both times it just rang and rang.

Oh well, I thought, she'll be back tomorrow.

Later that night Sammy asked me if he could try to get to one hundred baskets again the next day. He'd ended up with twenty-one.

"Sure," I said, "that can be your daily mission until you get it."

I was happy—it meant that I wouldn't have to think up new daily missions every day.

CHAPTER 12

Two more days passed and still Aleta didn't show up to the Secret Spot. On Sunday, I saw Raquel and her dad in church but Aleta wasn't with them.

"Where's Aleta?" I asked Raquel as the sermon came to an end and people stood to leave.

Raquel looked hesitantly at her father. He was standing with his back to us but I had a feeling he was listening. "She's not feeling well," she said.

"Oh," I said, not doing a very good job of hiding my disappointment.

"But if you want to call this evening I can make sure she picks up."

I shrugged. "Okay, I guess I could do that."

I had to fight to hold back my smile.

Later that evening when I spoke to Aleta, it didn't sound like she was sick—it sounded like she was sad. She barely said a word and most of the time I could just hear her sniffling in the background.

"Do you want to go to the spot tomorrow?" I asked, not using the word 'secret' because I was worried Sammy or my parents were listening from the other room.

"I don't think so," Aleta said quietly back.

"Why not?"

I got no reply.

"We could just go for a little while."

Again—no reply.

"Okay, I'm going to go. I guess I'll wait for a bit by the burnt tree and if you don't show up I'll just go by myself." I waited a long time to see if she'd say anything but she didn't. "Okay, well, see you tomorrow maybe."

I heard the phone click on the other end.

The next day I waited by the burnt tree just like I'd said. I waited for over an hour but Aleta never showed up. I felt angry. Why was she all of the sudden avoiding me? Hadn't we had fun together? She'd loved the Secret Spot—I knew that—so why had she stopped coming? If she was sad, wouldn't the Secret Spot make her feel better?

I ended up going to the pond by myself and reading for the day. I could've gone back and played with Sammy but I kept worrying Aleta might show up and I'd miss her. But she never came—not that day, or the next, or the next.

And when I'd return home from the pond each day I'd find Sammy in the driveway playing basketball, each time a little closer to one hundred.

"Thirty-four!" he called out as I approached through the backyard on the third day.

I gave him the thumbs up and we shot around for a bit before I headed inside. I was too miserable to play for very long.

After five days of reading and swimming alone at the Secret Spot, I was ready to give up. It wasn't the same without Aleta. It was boring. I thought about how I'd have to go back to playing with Sammy. He may not have been able to read or climb trees but at least he was reliable. Luckily, it never came to that, because on the sixth day I found Aleta waiting with her backpack in our usual meeting spot.

She was sitting with her back against the trunk wearing a white dress with daffodils and flip-flops instead of running shoes. I guess she had made the decision not to run and that was fine with me.

As I approached, I didn't make eye contact. I didn't even say hello. I wanted her to know I was mad. I wanted an apology but it didn't come—Aleta didn't say anything. She just studied me for a while before standing up and leading the way to the Secret Spot.

When we got there, I sat down in our usual spot beneath a maple with an above-ground root perfect for sitting and another smaller root that made an armrest. Normally Aleta sat next to me and we'd look through the goods we'd packed for the day but this time she walked straight past. She continued around the pond until she got to a maple tree on the edge of the hill and sat down beneath it. I pretended not to notice but I was beginning to feel really annoyed. After five days of being stood up, the last thing I wanted was to be ignored. I might as well have come alone.

I pulled out a *Goosebumps* book from my bag and opened it, but instead of reading I watched Aleta.

For a while she just stared at the lake, barely moving. She was like a statue made of stone and placed beneath the tree. Then the wind picked up and her dress ruffled and she quickly flattened it with her hands. That seemed to bring her back to the present and she looked around. When she looked at me I quickly turned my eyes back to my book, pretending to read. After a while she unzipped her backpack and reached inside, bringing out a book I'd never seen before. It wasn't a *Goosebumps* book, I could tell that much, but aside from that I didn't know what it was. There were no words on the cover and it looked to be made of black leather with some sort of design etched into it. I couldn't make out the design from across the pond.

Next, Aleta pulled out a pencil from her bag and sat tapping it against her bottom lip, looking out over the water like she was going to draw a picture of the landscape. But when she finally put her pencil to the paper, I could tell by way the pencil moved that she wasn't drawing—she was writing. And she was writing fast. She wrote for ten minutes straight without looking up. And as she did, her facial expressions changed. She started with the same blank stare she'd had all morning, but as she wrote, a thin smile seemed to cross her lips. At first I thought I was imagining it but then the smile grew and it became very clear it was a smile. Which was odd because the way the sun was reflecting off her face, I could see two shimmering streams beneath her eyes. She was crying—crying and smiling.

Watching her was agonizing. It was like watching someone telling a secret right in front of me—just to be annoying.

I'd had enough. I stood up and walked around the pond to where she was sitting.

Aleta saw me coming and shut the book quickly so that I didn't get to see what she was writing. The front cover design turned out to be flowers.

"What are you writing?" I asked.

She sat rubbing the front of the book with her hand, not saying anything.

I was getting madder. "Why are you ignoring me? What did I do to you?"

Aleta seemed startled by the force in my voice and looked up at me.

"I'm not," she said, "I mean, I'm sorry. It's nothing—I'm not writing anything."

"Oh, come on, it's not nothing. I saw that there was something written inside."

She sat thinking again for a while. "Okay, you're right, it's not nothing," she said.

"Then why can't you tell me what it is?"

"Because...it's...it's...it's none of your business," she said, holding the book to her chest like I might try to pry it away from her.

That did it. All the built up anger I'd had from six days of sitting alone at the pond came rushing out. "What is up with you?" I yelled. "You ditch me for a week and don't tell me why. Then we come here and you sit by yourself writing something like it's the most interesting thing in the world and won't tell me what it is. I don't understand you. I thought we were getting along great and now, I dunno, it's like you're some completely different person. Where were you all week?"

Aleta looked down at the book. "I wasn't feeling well," she whispered.

"That's not true!" I said, stamping my foot. "You weren't sick—you were sad. I could hear you crying when I called. And I saw you crying just now. Why won't you tell me what it is you're sad about? What's the big secret? Is it something to do with your parents? Is it about your mom?"

Aleta said nothing.

"I'm not leaving until you tell me. You can't just keep ignoring me."

Aleta looked up at me again but this time her eyes were red and tears were rolling down her cheeks like the day of our bike ride. She started shaking her head from side to side. "Not you too, Cal," she said. "Not you too."

"Not me too, what?" I asked.

"All day long, all I hear over and over, 'Aleta, tell me what you're thinking; tell me how you're feeling, tell me why you're sad.' You're right, Cal, I am sad, but I don't want to talk about it. There are some things that are easier not to talk about."

She turned her face away from me and wiped her eyes with the back of her hand.

I suddenly felt sorry for yelling. I realized I was only mad because I had missed her and this was just making things worse. I sat down beside her and put my chin on my knees. Beneath my hand, I felt a small pebble in the dirt and I picked it up and threw it into the pond, watching the ripples move outwards while I thought of what to say. I decided to keep it simple.

"I'm sorry."

"It's fine," she said. "I'm not trying to ignore you. I just wish there was somewhere I could go that I didn't have to talk to anyone about everything. Somewhere truly away from it all."

I thought for a moment, looking around. "Well," I said, gesturing around us to the vast expanse, "this could be that place. I mean this is our Secret Spot after all. You should feel safe here. I promise from now on I won't ask you any more questions about whatever it is you don't want to talk about. This place will only be for *Goosebumps*, mud-sliding, swimming and writing. No more questions."

Aleta looked over at me. Her face seemed hopeful.

"Do you mean that?" she asked.

"One hundred percent," I said, crossing my heart with my finger.

"You won't get annoyed with me writing and not telling you what it's about? You're not going to try to read over my shoulder?"

I shook my head emphatically.

"I promise I won't. As long as you promise not to ditch out on me anymore."

I held out my hand and Aleta shook it.

"Deal," she said, with a big smile.

Chapter 13

"*Welcome to Camp Nightmare* or *The Werewolf of Fever Swamp*?" Aleta asked, hopping over a small brook and landing neatly on the far side.

"*The Werewolf of Fever Swamp*," I replied, following Aleta's lead but managing to catch my heel in a soft spot of mud on the far side. "But they're both classics. Not like *Why I'm Afraid of Bees*. That's the worst. I mean, what's so scary about getting turned into a bee?" I pulled my foot from the mud and jogged to catch up as Aleta continued to march through the thick grass. "What about: *Go Eat Worms!* or *Say Cheese And Die!*?"

"*Say Cheese and Die!*" Aleta said without hesitation. "Nothing beats *Say Cheese and Die!*"

"Yeah, nothing beats *Say Cheese and Die!*" I agreed. And it was true—of all the *Goosebumps* books it was my favourite.

We had been hiking for over two hours and decided to play "which-*Goosebumps*-book-is-better" to occupy the time. I looked up ahead to see if we were any closer to Lake Huron only to be disappointed. It was like Lake Huron had legs and was walking away from us as we walked toward it.

"Ugh," I groaned, "we're not even close." I let my head fall backwards and closed my eyes, feeling the hot sun and hoping that

Aleta would agree that our goal of hiking to Lake Huron was futile.

Instead, I opened my eyes to see something hurtling toward my head and ducked just in time to avoid a thick clump of grass and dirt as it sailed by.

"What was that?" I exclaimed, looking over at Aleta to find her wiping her hands on her shorts.

She shrugged. "What was what?"

I stared at her and she tried her best not to smile but then she cracked and started to laugh. I looked around to try and find something to throw back but she was already running away.

Ever since I'd promised not to bug Aleta about what made her sad, it was like she'd opened right up, like she'd been a flower that had popped open in the spring. I found out her nervous, quiet, shy side was just a tactic to avoid questions she didn't want to answer. I knew because she still kept it up in church. She barely even said a word to me unless there was absolutely no one around—which was basically never at church.

At the Secret Spot she was different. She laughed, she joked, she'd play tricks on me whenever I let my guard down. If I ever got too absorbed in my book I could be sure that sooner or later a raisin or pebble or apple core would come flying my way. Luckily, her aim wasn't very good. We'd usually read and write for the morning until we'd grow bored and restless, then find something else to do for the afternoon. Sometimes Aleta would bring Chloe (we decided animals didn't count against the secret because there were already frogs and ducks and groundhogs at the pond) and we'd play hide-and-go-seek in the corn fields or watch Chloe chase bullfrogs by the pond. Other times we'd explore the woods beside the pond, hiking far enough to find a dilapidated shed at the end of a field. Inside there were old, rusty tools and a length of rope that we'd brought back to the Secret Spot to make a swing.

One day we'd been standing at the top of the hill when Aleta had said, "I bet we can hike all the way to Lake Huron."

I'd agreed, but I guess from the top of the hill things had looked closer because after two and half hours of hiking, I was fairly certain we weren't going to make it.

Part of the problem was the terrain. There was no clear path and the grass was tangled and knotted so that it grabbed at our feet and tripped us as we walked. Sometimes what seemed like solid ground was actually mossy bog and we'd have to circle around until we found a route where we could cross. There were groundhog holes, fallen branches, divots and mounds—it wasn't exactly a sidewalk or bike path.

"How about *Cuckoo Clock of Doom* or *The Haunted Mask*?" I asked.

Aleta gave a fake shiver. "*The Haunted Mask*! Definitely the creepiest ending to any *Goosebumps* book."

I laughed. "Yeah, I had to explain it to Sammy because he didn't get it. Then he talked about it for weeks. He was so scared he couldn't sleep."

I had been scared too.

"Which one is Sammy's favourite?"

I thought for a second. "Probably *Cuckoo Clock of Doom*," I said. "He likes the ending because he thinks the brother feels bad for making his little sister disappear. Except I'm pretty sure the brother isn't actually going to go back in time to rescue her."

My stomach started to feel funny.

It was a feeling I'd been getting every time Aleta brought up Sammy. For the most part, when I was with Aleta I hardly thought about my brother. But when I did, I'd start to get this feeling like I was suddenly hungry.

Except I knew it wasn't hunger—it was guilt.

As much as Aleta and I had grown closer, Sammy and I had grown apart.

For a while, he'd kept up with the basketball; determined to complete his daily mission.

Each day he got a little closer until one afternoon I'd come home to find him sitting on the basketball in the middle of the backyard waiting for me. He was practically vibrating he was so excited.

"One hundred!" he shrieked as soon as he saw me.

I made a big deal out of it and gave him his Badger Level, only to find out he didn't know what a Badger was, and since I didn't really know what one looked like either I had to make it up. For a short while things had seemed like they were back to normal but then later that night he'd asked me quietly in bed, "Cal, can I come with you and Aleta tomorrow?"

And I'd had to say no.

"Okay," he'd said in a sad little voice that had made my stomach hurt.

So, for the next few weeks he'd continued to play basketball and I'd continued to spend time with Aleta. Except when I'd come home in the afternoon there was no more excitement in his eyes, there were no more stories of his day, there were no more counts of how many baskets he'd sunk—just sad little eyes watching me walk past.

And my stomach would feel hungry.

Sad hungry.

It was sometime in early August that Mom had finally had enough.

I knew she was waiting for me the moment I opened the screen door to the kitchen. I saw her sitting at the table with eyes that said I'd done something wrong.

I tried to walk past. I tried to avoid the look.

"Calvin," she said, using my full name, which was never a good sign. "I need to talk with you."

I knew what the talk was going to be about. She'd hinted at it a few times over the weeks before when she'd asked, "Where are you going? Is Sammy going with you?"

But Dad had intervened. "Oh, leave the boy alone. I seem to recall another love-struck couple spending more than their fair share of time sneaking off when they were just getting to know each other."

Then he'd wrap his arms around Mom and her serious face would melt and I would be allowed to slip away without a lecture.

But on this particular day, Dad wasn't there to bail me out.

Mom started every lecture with the same question.

"What do you think I want to talk about?" she asked, her eyes narrow and piercing.

So I went through my usual rigmarole of playing dumb. Normally it was something like, "Is it the fact that I'm wearing my shoes inside?" when really I knew it was the black mark on the back deck I'd left when I'd tried to teach Sammy how to light a campfire.

That day it was, "Umm, did I leave my pajamas on the floor?"

"Calvin," she said, looking over my shoulder, "look at your brother."

I turned around to see Sammy doing what he'd been doing endlessly for the last few weeks—shooting the basketball.

"He's getting better, huh?" I said.

He was. In the few seconds I watched, he made both his shots.

"I'm not talking about that. I'm talking about the fact that he's been all alone for the last three weeks shooting that basketball so that he can impress you and you come home and barely acknowledge him." I considered telling her that he wasn't shooting to impress me but I didn't want to divulge any information about the Levels. After an uncomfortable few seconds, she continued, "Your father and I agreed to give you some time to get to know Aleta. We understand that it's nice to have friends your own age and I'm happy you're getting along so well but look at Sammy—he misses you. There is no one to play with when you're gone and Dad is at work. Can't you take him with you?"

I groaned. "Mommmm, it's so lame that I have to take my brother with me. And besides, Aleta might not want him around. And it's a really long walk to the Secret Spot."

"The Secret Spot?" Mom asked.

Crust—I'd accidentally let it slip.

"Well, it's not actually a Secret Spot," I said, backtracking. "It's just...It's just..."

There was no obvious explanation that came to mind. Everything I said would either get me in trouble for being selfish or give Mom too much information about our Secret Spot.

"Please, Calvin," Mom said, "he looks up to you so much. It may not seem like it right now, but when you're older, you're going to realize how important he is."

I fidgeted with my shirt not looking directly at her but I knew she wasn't going anywhere until I said yes. I slouched my shoulders, I rolled my eyes, I groaned as dramatically as I could. I wanted Mom to feel like I was doing her a really big favour but deep down I knew she was right.

"Fiiiine. I'll take him with me tomorrow," I said, stomping out of the kitchen and up the stairs to my room.

I thought about what I'd tell Aleta the next day when I brought Sammy. Deep down I knew she wouldn't care but I wanted her to care. I wanted her to feel protective over our Secret Spot. I wanted it so badly that I started to convince myself that she would care. I started to worry about how I would tell her the news.

But then the next morning, I found out that all my worrying was for nothing. Sammy was still in bed long after I'd finished breakfast and Mom went up to check on him. When she came back down, she had a worried expression.

"Sammy's not feeling well again. I think his fevers are back," she said to Dad.

Dad shook his head slowly. "Poor kid. It's been a rough summer. Another cold probably."

"I'm worried it's not just a cold."

"Let's give it a day or two and we can bring him back to Dr. Whatever-His-Name-Is and have him take another look."

"I'm going to call the doctor now and see if he can see him today," Mom said, walking over to the phone.

"You know, I'm sort of a doctor myself," Dad joked. "Remember the piece I wrote last year on medical errors? I had to interview more than a few white-coats and basically got my MD."

"I'm not joking, Harold."

Dad shrugged and went back to his reading. "Okay, suit yourself, take him in. But make sure they give him the banana-flavoured stuff. And ask them to pack seconds for me."

Mom hung up the phone disappointed.

"They're not open yet," she said with a huff.

She started to walk out of the kitchen to go back upstairs.

"Mom, does this mean I don't have to take Sammy with me?" I asked.

"Not today," she said.

Three more weeks had passed and I still hadn't had to take Sammy to the Secret Spot. It was the last week of August and already the air was starting to change. The hot mugginess of summer had left and there was a cool bite to the breeze as it passed. A few of the farmers had been plowing their fields as I'd walked to the Secret Spot that morning. Soon the towering corn would be nothing more than dirt and grass.

"Can you believe school is less than a week away?" I said, catching up to Aleta as she stood on the top of a dirt hill looking out toward the lake. It had been another hour and we still weren't any closer. "I really don't think we're going to make it," I said, following her gaze.

I looked at Aleta and saw she looked worried. I guess making it to Lake Huron was a bigger deal than I'd thought.

"We could always try again tomorrow," I said. "Start earlier or something."

The wind picked up, blowing Aleta's hair over her face but she didn't seem to notice. She was thinking about something.

"We can keep going," I said. "I was just saying that it's getting a little late in the afternoon but if you really want to keep going we can probably make it."

"No," she said, "we should turn around. I was just thinking about school, that's all."

I felt relieved that we weren't going to keep hiking.

"Don't worry about school. The homework isn't that hard, and I can help you."

"I'm not worried about the homework," she said.

"Then what are you worried about?"

"I don't know, everything I guess—the kids, the teachers, the thought of going back to school. When I left Ryerson in London, things weren't so great."

"You're worried about people asking you questions," I said.

Aleta looked at me, holding my eyes for a moment. She nodded. "Yeah, that too."

"I'll sit with you on the bus and if anyone asks you anything, I'll knock 'em square in the kisser."

Aleta laughed. "The kisser?"

"It's what my dad says. But seriously, I'll make sure no one bugs you. It'll be fine."

"Thanks, Cal—you're a great friend. I've never had a friend like you."

"Me neither," I said. "I've never had a friend like me either."

We both laughed and turned back toward the pond.

Chapter 14

On the first day of school, Mom took me aside in the morning for another "talk." She pulled me into the living room while Dad and Sammy ate their breakfasts and I figured I was in trouble. Except usually I knew what I'd done—this time I wasn't sure.

"I'm worried about Sammy," she said. "He's still not feeling well but he's too excited to stay home. Can you promise me that you'll keep an eye on him today?"

It was true. Sammy had been doing his best all morning to pretend he was well. He'd gotten up early, brushed his teeth, dressed and packed his lunch (which Mom had to repack)—all before I'd even gotten out of bed. Except when I'd climbed down from my bunk, I'd seen his sheets were drenched with sweat, so I knew he was still having fevers. The doctor had said Sammy had something called mono and that it would take him a few weeks to get over it.

"If he still isn't feeling well why not just keep him home?" I argued. "Why does he have to be my responsibility?"

I was feeling a little nervous about my first day back at Huxbury too and didn't want to have to watch out for Sammy. I already had Aleta to worry about.

Mom gave me an angry glare.

"Okay, okay, sure—I'll watch out for Sammy," I said.

In the kitchen, I found Dad and Sammy sitting at the table. Dad was eating and reading the paper while Sammy sat beside him looking nervous. His eyes were ringed with dark circles and he was wearing his new pants and shirt Mom had got him from our back-to-school shopping. Although, Sammy had needed more than just back to school shopping that summer. He'd lost a lot of weight, which I figured was a combination of playing so much basketball, not baking as much and being sick all the time.

Sammy already had his backpack on, even though the bus wouldn't be there for another hour and it looked like he hadn't taken more than a couple bites of his cereal.

"You ready for today?" I asked, sitting down beside him. Mom had put a bowl of cereal out for me but had forgotten a spoon so I grabbed Sammy's—he was done anyway.

Sammy nodded.

I took a big bite of my cereal then proceeded to talk with my mouth full. "Don't worry," I said, as milk dripped to the table. "Grade two is a breeze. All you have to do is read, like, one book or something and you pass."

Sammy didn't seem relieved.

"They're easy books. Not like *Goosebumps* or anything. You'll be fine."

Dad put down his paper. "And don't forget that they have all-you-can-eat gumball machines and a servant that walks around to your desks and says, 'Can I get you some more gumballs, good sir?'"

Sammy smiled. "No, they don't," he said, then glanced at me to make sure Dad was joking.

"Not gumball machines—ice cream machines," I said, joining in. "With every flavour you could possibly imagine and a little tube that sticks out of your desk so you can just suck it back while you listen to the teacher."

"And flying carpets for chairs," Dad said.

"All right, enough, you two," Mom interjected. "We don't want him showing up on his first day asking where the ice cream machines are."

"I know they're joking," Sammy said. He was smiling and his nervous look was gone.

After breakfast, Sammy and I waited by the front door for the bus. When we saw it coming down the road, I bolted only to hear Mom yell, "Calvin, get back here!"

I stopped, turned around, went back and gave her a quick hug. I was about to start running again when I remembered our conversation from earlier. I waited for Sammy to give her a hug too—which was very long and drawn out—then grabbed his hand and started to walk down the driveway. I knew Mom would appreciate the handhold.

When we got on the bus, it was mostly empty and I walked down the aisle and took a seat somewhere in the middle. Sammy followed and sat down next to me, hugging his backpack and not saying a word.

The very next stop was Aleta's house and as we turned onto Thornton Road I saw her standing next to Raquel at the end of their driveway. She was wearing a long, black pea coat and her hair was neatly pulled up into a ponytail. Her shoes looked shiny and new and she wasn't wearing a backpack, but rather, a leather satchel thing that hung over one shoulder. She looked really proper and fashionable—not like the other kids we would be picking up.

"Sammy, move over," I said, giving him a little shove and pointing across the aisle to another empty seat.

He looked confused, then looked out the window at Aleta, then back at me, then got up and moved across the aisle without arguing.

Aleta got on and looked nervously around. She reminded me of a cornered mouse as her eyes frantically darted around the bus.

"Aleta," I said, giving a wave, "over here."

She saw me and quickly made her way back and sat down next to me. She didn't say a word and I knew from her body language she wasn't interested in talking. As the bus continued along the road and more nervous kids got on, I quietly whispered who they were and whether they were nice or funny or annoying or whatever else I could think to tell Aleta.

A few stops later, we pulled up to a small, rundown farmhouse with a cluttered lawn and two figures hunched by the road. One was kneeling behind the other rummaging through a backpack. Behind the screen door, I saw the silhouette of a man smoking. The two figures by the road looked back and gave the briefest of waves before climbing on the bus. The man in the doorway didn't wave back but watched for a moment longer before opening the screen door to throw out his cigarette then heading back inside. I knew this house well and never looked forward to the stop.

Tom and Joey walked down the aisle with mischievous grins. They climbed into the seat in front of Aleta and me, facing backwards despite my attempt to avoid eye contact. Their faces were dirty and it was apparent they hadn't bathed in a while.

"I seen you in church," Tom declared as he stared at Aleta. I could feel her discomfort as she looked down at her feet. "What's your name?"

Aleta didn't answer. Instead she continued to look down. I knew this would only antagonize Tom and he leaned in closer, the smell of cigarettes on his jacket suffocating us in our seat. I felt a rapidly developing situation in which I'd probably have to do something when Joey yelled, "Wow, Pudge lost weight!" from across the aisle.

Tom looked over to find Sammy slouched down low in his seat, trying to go unnoticed.

He moved across the aisle and joined his brother. "Did he ever!" he said, his voice intentionally loud as to attract the attention of the entire bus. "What, your family can't feed ya or some'n?"

Tom got a few laughs from around the bus at this. It was ironic because everyone knew the Rileys were dirt poor. I stayed quiet. The less you said, the less they bothered you—for the most part. "You know we still gonna call you Pudge, right? 'Cept now maybe we'll call ya Twiggy Pudge."

More laughs.

Tom and Joey continued picking on Sammy for a while before getting bored and moving on to some other kid. Our school went to grade six before kids moved across the road to junior high—grade seven and eight—and those kids had their own bus. That meant Tom—and I—were the oldest kids now, which meant there were no kids to tell Tom to shut up. By the time we'd arrived at the school, everyone had had enough of the Rileys.

We pulled up in front of the old red brick building marked 'Uxbury Elementary' across the front. The 'H' in Huxbury had fallen off the year before and fixing it apparently hadn't made the list of to-dos over the summer.

As we all hurried to get off the bus, Sammy stumbled on the stairs and bumped into the kid in front of him.

"Watch it!" the kid said, turning around. He was bigger than Sammy, but not bigger than me.

"You watch it," I said from behind Sammy and the kid looked up at me. His angry sneer faded and he turned and walked quickly away.

Sammy looked back at me. He had a worried look on his face but there was something else—something I couldn't quite place. It reminded me of the time he'd fallen off his bike on our ride with Aleta. He looked dazed or out of it or something.

"You okay?" I asked.

His eyes focused in on my face and he nodded.

"All right," I said, looking around. "You're over there with Ms. Wincott," I pointed to where a short lady with glasses stood with a clipboard and a sign that said, Grade Two. "See you at lunch?"

Sammy nodded again and made his way toward the line of grade two kids. I noticed Joey at the front making faces at the kid behind him. God, I hated that kid.

I grabbed Aleta by the sleeve and led her through the mob toward the grade six door. I smiled when I saw the teacher—Ms. Draper, the grade six teacher from the year before. She had supervised lunch on occasion and was really nice. I was even more pleased when I learned later that Aleta and I would have desks right beside each other. Everything was working out.

Tom was put at the front of the class, which I suspected wasn't an accident, and we spent the morning going over the usual stuff—introductions, where our lockers were, what our classes would be.

When the bell rang for lunch, the whole school scrambled for the playground. Every group had their own area—older girls in the corner by the main building, younger kids either playing tag in the field or basketball on the lower nets, older boys on the two higher nets. Someone grabbed a ball from the bin and we were ready to get started. I saw Sammy walking toward the lower net slowly with his head down. Mom's voice echoed in my head for a fleeting second before I turned to the more pressing matters of organizing teams. As Aleta hadn't made friends yet, she stood by the court watching.

It wasn't a particularly warm day, but once we started playing it felt hot. Tom obviously had been practicing over the summer because his dribbling was noticeably better. I was disappointed when the ball bounced off my leg on more than one occasion and went out of bounds. I did my best not to look at Aleta who continued to watch us.

We stopped for a brief water break between games and as I walked to the fountain I watched the younger kids playing bump. The game involved a line of kids trying to get the ball in before the person behind them. If they didn't, they were out. There were now only three kids left and Sammy was one of them. Joey was another. Evidently my daily missions had improved his shot because for the minute I stood watching, he didn't miss once. Around and around the last three went, each making their shots, not able to get the others out. Finally, Joey managed to grab the basketball of the third and smallest of the remaining three boys and smash it with his own so that it went hurtling across the playground. Snickering as the boy chased the ball, he casually turned toward the basket and waited. By the time the boy had grabbed his ball and was running back, Joey tossed his ball up and through the hoop and the other boy was out.

"Thought I'd give you a chance to get back," Joey said with a laugh as the boy walked off the court.

My own game was on hold while everyone stood watching the last two younger kids. I saw Sammy look over at me briefly with a hint of a smile on his face before turning toward the basket and making his shot. A half second later, Joey's ball followed and had Sammy missed he would have been out. Again and again they went, neither missing before finally Joey's ball struck rim and bounced away. It was Sammy's chance to finish him off but he was bent over gasping for breath under the net. The crowd of kids was now cheering and everyone yelled at Sammy to run back to the free throw line. By the time he waddled to the line, Joey had retrieved his ball and was running back.

"Hurry up!" I heard myself shout.

Sammy turned toward the basket and threw the ball with what appeared to be all the strength he had left. The ball seemed to freeze in every frame as it made its way toward the net. Up, down, swish—the ball passed through the rim just before Joey managed to get back for an easy layup. The crowd erupted into cheers and Joey's face turned crimson.

I was ready to run over and high-five my little brother when I saw him step back, stumble, then drop. I could tell by the way he fell that something wasn't right. It wasn't like when someone tripped—there was something different. It came to me. Normally, when someone falls they put out a hand or leg to catch themselves. Sammy just fell, like he was some doll tossed aside. There was no arm to brace the impact; there was no attempt to catch himself; there was nothing but the crack of his head hitting the pavement.

For the briefest of moments, Sammy lay perfectly still before his body starting moving. Only it wasn't moving normally—it was thrashing and jerking and flailing like nothing I'd ever seen.

Things started happening fast. Kids were yelling. Teachers came running and pushed the crowd aside as they fought to get next to Sammy.

"Clear out, we need room here!" a teacher yelled over the cries of worried children.

"Someone call an ambulance!" another yelled.

I fought my way through the crowd too—pushing and pulling at shirts and arms to get closer. Finally, I was able to see him. Sammy, my brother, eyes lifelessly rolling around; still open but not seeing.

"Is he okay?!" I screamed. "Is he okay?!"

It was a stupid question.

"Clear everyone out of here!" one of the teachers yelled and I felt strong arms pulling us back. I fought hard to stay near the front. I fought hard but I wasn't strong enough. I was pulled back with the crowd as two of the teachers knelt beside Sammy frantically trying to stop him from shaking.

"He's my brother!" I yelled, trying to break free as they herded us into the main building. "He's my brother!"

CHAPTER 15

BEFORE THAT DAY I HAD NEVER BEEN IN A HOSPITAL—ASIDE FROM being born, I guess.

Dad and I sat in the emergency waiting room. We were told by Dr. Mitchell—a tall man with a big nose and short hair—to wait while they got Sammy into a room.

I looked around the waiting room. It was full. Every seat held someone sitting and waiting. Across the room, a boy about my age sat holding his arm to his chest while his mom rubbed his back. His baseball uniform was dirty and ripped. I had never broken a bone in my whole life, or even had a cavity for that matter. I was always lucky like that.

Two seats down from him, a lady sat with a baby in her lap. The baby was crying as she rocked it back and forth in her arms. I couldn't imagine being that small. I could barely remember kindergarten. My earliest memories were from grade one when Sammy, still a toddler, was learning to walk and speak. I remembered holding his hand on the way to school and begging my mom to let me bring him in for Show and Tell.

After an eternity of sitting and watching people go in and out, it was our turn. A lady in what looked like pink pajamas led us down a white hallway decorated with cartoon characters on the walls—Mickey, Pluto, Donald Duck—all smiling and looking happy, masking the reality that hid behind every door. Sick children—sick children like Sammy.

When we arrived at Sammy's room Dad rushed in and grabbed Mom's hand where she sat next to a tired, pale Sammy. There was something ominous about that simple gesture that made me worried. I couldn't place it exactly, but something didn't feel right—as if they knew something I didn't.

The room was simple—a bed, three chairs, a sink and a bedside table on wheels. Behind the bed, tubing and wires went in every direction like roots from a tree. Sammy's finger glowed red and a wire led from it to a machine that blinked and beeped. Numbers flashed on a screen that I couldn't hope to understand.

I stood pretending to take in the room but was really thinking of what to say. I didn't want to let on how scared I was but the image of Sammy's flailing body on the playground kept repeating in my head.

Finally, after a long, awkward pause I said, "Hey, Sammy, sorry you're not feeling good."

I walked over to the bed and gave him a playful punch in the arm.

"Cal!" Mom said from her seat next to him.

"Oops, sorry."

I remember being struck by how white Sammy looked. The sheets were only slightly paler and his cheeks looked hollow, his eyes sunken and dark.

"Hey, Cal," he said back.

"Sammy played one heck of a game today," I said, half to my parents, half to Sammy. "He beat Joey and all the other kids in his grade. I was pretty sure Joey was going to punch you square in the face before you..." I trailed off. I didn't know how exactly to describe what I'd seen and I felt pretty sure Sammy wasn't in the mood to talk about it. "Anyway, I brought cards if you want to play Crazy Eights or something."

Mom gave me a look that said, "He's tired, we should let him sleep." She looked tired herself.

"I'm okay. We can play," Sammy argued, but his voice sounded frail and he didn't attempt to sit up in the bed.

Just then, the door opened and a short, chubby lady walked in. Her blond hair was tied in a messy braid and she was humming under her breath. She smiled at us as she set down a plastic bin on the bedside table.

"How's it going, love? You feeling any better?" she asked Sammy. "It's time to do your blood work. It will only take a minute." She motioned for me to slide down the bed and sat next to Sammy, "You've got your whole family with you, I see."

Mom and Dad introduced themselves. The lady said she was Sammy's nurse.

"And you must be the big brother," she said, looking at me. "You guys look so alike."

I cringed. Why did people keep insisting we looked so alike? Especially when—at that moment—Sammy looked more like the Grim Reaper than himself.

As the nurse prepared the needle, I felt myself getting queasy. I hated needles. Not that anyone really likes them, but I'd go so far as saying I had a phobia. I remembered back to when I had to get my Hep B shots in grade, what was it? Three? And the nurses that came in said it wouldn't hurt a bit. Well, it hadn't. I'd passed out in the chair at the sight of the needle and never felt a thing. It's not that uncommon—or so they told me.

Mom looked over at me. I must have taken on a colour similar to Sammy's because she asked if I was going to be okay.

The nurse stopped what she was doing and looked at me too. "Yeah, are you going to be okay? If you want to look away that's fine."

I shook my head and kept watching.

The nurse continued preparing. She opened a small package and wiped Sammy's arm with what looked like a Wet-Nap you get in restaurants. She tied a thick rubber band around his small bicep and prodded with her fingers in his elbow crease. After a couple seconds, she seemed content with what she'd felt and drew the needle. I wanted to look away but couldn't. It was like a car crash that everyone stops to watch. As the needle passed through the skin, I felt the metallic taste in my mouth as if I was going to be sick. A thin tube ran from the needle to a plastic container and that container started to fill with blood. All this time, Sammy continued to lie with his eyes closed. He didn't even flinch as the needle went in. I reminded myself to give him a Level when we got home.

The nurse finished up and turned to us before leaving the room "One of the doctors will be in soon to ask you some questions."

"Soon," I would learn, has a very different meaning in hospitals than it does elsewhere. Forty minutes later and still no one had shown up.

I tried to occupy my mind by daydreaming. I forced myself to think of Aleta and our Secret Spot but the images would only flutter in my mind briefly before those of Sammy's body on the playground concrete would force their way back in. He was sleeping and I considered waking him. Did it hurt? Do you remember it? Could you hear us yelling your name? All these questions lay unanswered, gnawing at me. The longer it went on, the worse it became.

Finally, a short, skinny Asian boy came in and introduced himself as Simon the Clinical Clerk.

"What's a clinical clerk?" Dad asked.

"It's a medical student in third year. I'm training to be a doctor," he replied.

"Medical school? Are you sure you're not still in high school?" Dad joked. The boy shook his head. "Well, Doogie Howser, let's get started. What's going on with my favourite son?" Dad winked at me as he said this.

"I'm not really sure yet, I—we—just need to get some information first," he said.

"Ignore my husband. He doesn't have an off button for his joking around," Mom said, shaking her head at Dad. "Go ahead with your questions."

The boy looked down at his clipboard where he obviously had a list because he rarely looked up from that point on.

"Okay, so what exactly happened today?"

Mom looked at me, "I think Cal can probably answer that question best."

I recounted in great detail the events that occurred on the basketball court leading up to the falling backwards, "And then, and then, he just sort of fainted but instead of lying still, his arms and legs were going crazy and his eyes were open and looking all over the place."

"How long did that shaking go on?"

"I dunno, a few minutes. There was a big crowd and the teachers were pushing us out of the way."

After some more jotting down on his clipboard, "And has he ever had a seizure like that before?"

"Seizure? What's a seizure?" I asked.

"No," Mom said, taking over from there.

"Had he been sick before the game?"

"He's been sick all summer. Our family doctor said he thought it was mono," Mom replied.

"Okay, we'll come back to that. Has he fallen lately? Hit his head at all?"

"No."

"Anyone in the family with epilepsy or a seizure disorder?"

"No."

"Any other health issues that Sammy has? Medications he's taking? Allergies?"

"No. No. No."

Simon seemed to be thinking as he stared at his clipboard.

"Any recent history of weight loss?"

"Yes, he has lost some weight over the summer."

"Any fevers?"

"Daily."

"Any night sweats?"

I thought back to all the mornings where I'd seen the swimming pool that was Sammy's bed.

"Yes."

"Any history of easy bruising?"

At this, Mom paused and looked at me, "He has had a lot of

bruises this summer, but his brother can be a bit rough with him, so I don't know about easy bruising."

I rolled my eyes.

"How has his energy level been?"

"Very poor. He's been napping nearly every day."

We sat in that room answering Simon the Clinical Clerk's questions for well over an hour. Any problems when you were pregnant with him? Issues with the delivery? Shortly after the delivery? Travelled anywhere recently? Anyone else sick? Any pets at home? Any of the following short list of signs or symptoms: diarrhea, constipation, obstipation, shortness of breath, chest pain, belly pain, joint pain, bone pain, lumps or bumps, rashes, runny nose, cough or menstrual irregularity. The list was apparently all-inclusive because at this last one Simon looked up, red in the face, and said, "Oops, sorry."

"Okay." Simon put his clipboard down. "I need to examine the patient."

"I'm sure *Sammy* would be happy to oblige," Dad answered.

Simon fumbled awkwardly with a device on the wall, dropping it once, before wrapping what looked like a black strap around Sammy's arm. He listened with his stethoscope while inflating what I now saw was some sort of balloon. When he was satisfied with what he'd done, he went back to his clipboard and scribbled more notes, never telling us what he was doing or what he thought.

"Stand up and walk across the room," Simon said.

"You didn't say, 'Simon-says,'" Dad joked.

Sammy tried to get out of bed but couldn't, so Dad went over to help. He managed to get Sammy up standing but he was wobbly and still didn't look like he was back to himself.

"Okay, never mind, we can just do the exam sitting," Simon said.

Sammy lay back down and Simon put him through a series of tasks that reminded me of some sort of game: take a breath, open your mouth, turn your head, touch your nose.

At the end of everything, Simon left the room without saying a word. We were all left a little stunned and Dad was chuckling to himself in the corner. "I suppose you don't need to have personality to become a doctor," he said.

The nurse who'd drawn Sammy's blood came back in with two popsicles. "It'll be another few minutes before the doctor is back, thought you'd like one of these in the meantime," she said, handing us each one.

Dr. Mitchell came back thirty minutes later, followed closely behind by Simon and his pet clipboard. He appeared hurried and spoke with hardly any pauses. "I can't say exactly what's going on with Sammy but I had a look through his blood test results and I think he's going to have to be admitted."

"Admitted?" I asked.

"Yes, he's going to have to stay in the hospital overnight, and possibly for the next few days while we run some tests to figure out what's going on."

I looked over at Sammy who appeared more interested in finishing his popsicle than the conversation around him.

"Wait, wait, slow down," Dad said. "What did his blood tests show?"

"He's anemic and thrombocytopenic. I can't say why, and it doesn't explain his seizure so I think it's best to admit him and see if they can figure it out."

Anemic? Thrombocytopenic?

The first word seemed vaguely familiar but the second didn't even sound English.

Dad seemed to be getting frustrated. "Look, can you just tell us in plain English what you think is going on here. I don't care if you can't say exactly, but you must have some idea."

Dr. Mitchell exhaled and sat down on the side of Sammy's bed. He proceeded to speak at an exaggeratedly slow pace as if we were all hard of hearing.

"Sammy had a seizure. Think of the brain as a cupboard full of wires. Normally, you open the cupboard and find nice, laid out sets of wires that send signals in a coordinated fashion. A seizure occurs when those wires get all jumbled and start firing in all different directions. What you saw—the thrashing movement, eyes rolling around—is the result of that. So that much we know: Sammy had a seizure. But a seizure is a symptom, not a diagnosis, meaning it tells us something is wrong inside, but not what is wrong. There are many things that cause a seizure—dehydration, low blood sugar, electrolyte abnormalities, infections—many things. Even fever itself can cause a seizure, except I'm worried there's something more going on here. I'm worried about what has been going on this summer. The weight loss, the bruising, the sweating; I know you were told it was likely mono but I think there's something more than mono going on here."

"What do you mean, something more than mono?" Mom asked.

"I mean that fevers and weight loss and fatigue can all be from mono, true, but after two months of fevers I think we need to start thinking of other things. That's why we're going to have Sammy stay overnight in the hospital. In the morning we'll run a few more tests and have the specialists see him."

"In the morning?" I blurted out. "But Sammy's sick now! Why can't the specialists see him now?"

"He's sick, but not critical. We can wait until morning. Nothing will have changed by then and it would be good to get some rest. It's been a long day for all of you. The room on the unit he's going to has a bed for someone to stay, but only one. The rest of you will have to come back tomorrow."

Sammy hadn't said a word during the whole discussion and now sat with his eyes half closed, remnants of an unfinished popsicle staining the white sheets at his side. The words 'more than mono' kept reverberating in my head while the image of the plastic tube filling with blood stained the inside of my eyelids. At least the image of the flailing had competition. My mind had become a haunted house straight out of a *Goosebumps* book.

I stayed awake for most of the ride home, but somewhere along the dark highway between the small towns of Ontario I must have fallen asleep because I don't remember how I got into bed; only the frequent awakenings that followed.

Chapter 16

The next morning I heard Dad talking on the phone in a hushed voice as I walked into the kitchen. I still felt tired despite the sun already creeping over the tree line.

"All right, that sounds good. Yes, I'll be in as soon as I've dropped him off."

He put the phone back on the receiver and smiled at me.

"Good news. Your brother is doing well. Turns out they won't have to amputate his head after all," he said.

"That's disappointing," I joked.

He laughed then his face took on a somewhat more serious look as he told me "they"—which I knew meant "Mom"—thought it was best for me to go to school and be picked up after.

"That's not fair!" I argued. "I want to come and see how Sammy's doing."

"And you will, just as soon as school is over. One of us will be back to pick you up at six pm sharp."

"School's done at four."

"Then we won't be a minute later than five," Dad said with a grin.

"Ugh, this is so unfair. And I've already missed the bus in case you hadn't noticed."

I marched out of the kitchen, stomping my feet for effect.

It's one thing to walk into class late, it's another to walk into class late the day after your brother had an epic attack of jerking and foaming and flailing. Since nothing exciting ever happened at recess, on the rare occasion that a fight broke out or someone slipped and needed stitches, those trivial events were talked about for days. I could only imagine how long people would be talking about Sammy's seizure.

An awkward silence fell over the class as I walked toward my desk next to Aleta. She turned toward me with a worried look on her face. Everyone was looking at me as if I were going to make some sort of public announcement. Even Ms. Draper paused for me to take my seat, then seemed to hesitate before going on with the class.

I sat with my chin on my hands pretending to listen but instead kept thinking about Sammy. I'd never really worried about him before. Even when he'd been sick over the summer. But something about the fall and the hospital and the worried looks on my parents' faces—it was all so unnerving. I couldn't shake the feeling. He'd be fine, I knew he'd be fine, but crust, what if he wasn't? I had to shake my head a few times to get rid of the thought.

The worrying was one thing, dealing with everyone in my class who seemed to think Sammy's health was their business was another. I would close my eyes briefly, then open them again, each time hoping that when I did everything would be back to normal. Aleta would stop looking at me with her worried eyes, Tom would stop turning around every chance he got with a smug sneer on his face, and Ms. Draper would stop trying to catch my eye while she talked. I wished they'd all just stop. The tension in the room was unbearable and the closer to lunch it got, the more I wanted to run out of the portable and never come back.

I knew it would be a free-for-all come recess. I thought about playing sick but knew that would only make it worse later. I told myself it was better to just face everyone then and there and get it over with. I tried to convince myself that it was all in my head and that no one would make a big deal of it but sure enough, come recess, Tom and Joey headed the pack of kids waiting outside the portable door when the bell rang. They formed a ring, preventing me from walking around, so I stood and waited with what I hoped was a "What do you want?" look on my face.

"Hey, Cal, where's your brother at?" Tom jeered as I walked toward them. "Did they put him in a crazy jacket when they took'm to the loony bin?" He flexed his wrists and held them stiffly to his face while making jerking movements with his body. A few kids from the group laughed.

"God, that was the funniest thing we ever seen," Joey joined in. "We were up all night laugh'n 'bout it. Every time we thought we's just about done, we'd crack up all over again." He awkwardly attempted to imitate his older brother.

I felt my fingers curl into tight fists as I took a step toward them. I had never punched anyone but my brother before—and that was always in fun—but I had a feeling that right then and there that was about to change. And I'm sure it would have, if, at that moment, one of the teachers, Mr. O'Byrne, hadn't come roaring into the crowd. The sea of students parted like corn stalks in the wind and formed a trail right to Tom and Joey.

"Tom, Joey, principal's, now!" he barked.

It didn't matter. They had an audience and the principal's office was nothing new for the Riley brothers. They kept on taunting until their heads disappeared through the door of the main building.

I was seething by that point and ready to lash out at the next person who said anything. I glared around at the rest of the group but they weren't interested in following Joey and Tom. The crowd dispersed, leaving me standing alone, angry, hurt, wanting to scream but afraid my voice would break.

Aleta stood a few feet away watching me breathe in and out slowly as I attempted to regain some composure. She walked over and stood beside me.

She didn't say anything but she didn't have to—just having her next to me made me feel a little better and after a while I felt myself calming down. We spent recess standing together, watching the boys play basketball and the girls skipping as everyone else pretended not to be looking at me. And I pretended not to notice when they glanced over and whispered to the kid beside them. The talking would go on for a long time, it was something I would get used to, but it would take a while.

Just before the end of recess, I saw a car pull up in front of the school and Mr. Riley got out. He looked in a huff as he headed into the school and I nudged Aleta. A few minutes later he walked back out, one of each of the Rileys in his thick hands, holding them tightly behind the neck so that their feet were barely on the ground. He yanked the car door open and in went the boys—toss, toss—like limp sacks of feed. I only just caught a glimpse of Tom's face as he sat slumped in the backseat. He wasn't laughing anymore.

CHAPTER 17

After school I found Mom sitting in the car at the front of the school with her eyes closed. I'd expected a lengthy discussion on what the doctors had found and what they'd decided to do, but it turned out that not much had happened throughout the day. Mom spoke slowly and I realized she likely hadn't slept much in the last twenty-four hours as she kept losing track of what she was saying and starting over.

"It's been slow so far. Just a bunch of telling and retelling what happened yesterday to various doctors," she said.

"Which doctors, Mom? Who?" I asked.

"I can hardly keep track of them all. Let's see, there was a Dr. what-was-his-name, a nice man with a bowtie, Dr. Sommerville, the neurologist. He's a brain doctor. They want to do a test called an EEG. They might have already done it by the time we get there. And the infectious disease doctors came by, apparently they deal with all the bacteria and infections kids get. They said they could do some tests to see if Sammy has mono. They drew some more blood. We've had lunch and we're waiting for dinner. Sammy's looking better. He slept through the night. He's looking forward to seeing you. He keeps asking when you're getting there."

We entered the hospital through the main entrance, which was a lot nicer than the emergency waiting room. Large sliding doors opened to a wide foyer. A sign on the wall read, Please Wash Your Hands, and a hand sanitizer pump hung below it. I watched my mom pump clear gel into her hands, rubbing it around so it disappeared and dried like magic. I did the same, then followed her as she walked through the lobby. She walked quickly and I struggled to keep up as I looked around. To my right, a large tank full of coral and exotic fish, to my left, the monotonous drone of voices and dishes clattering in the cafeteria, ahead, the elevators.

Unit 31—General Pediatrics, the sign read as we got off on the third floor. Sammy's room looked similar to the one in the emergency department but it was less plain and had a TV at the end of his bed.

I nearly laughed when I first saw Sammy. He looked like something straight out of a horror movie. He was awake and less pale than the day before but his head was wrapped in one of those turban things certain people wear. At the top of the turban, wires shot out like branches.

"What is that thing?" I laughed, walking up to him.

"It's called an EEG," an unfamiliar voice said.

I nearly jumped. I hadn't noticed the man sitting in the chair beside Sammy's bed as I'd walked in.

"It measures the brainwaves in his head to make sure everything is firing correctly."

His voice was deep but gentle and his white, fluffy hair reminded me of Santa Claus. Come to think of it, a lot about Dr. Parker made me think of Santa Claus. I remember liking him the moment I met him.

He stood up from the chair and shook Mom's hand. She seemed equally surprised to see him.

"I'm Dr. Parker. Please, come in and sit down. I've just been talking with Sammy and your husband. It turns out Sammy and I have the same birthday and we were just bouncing ideas off each other about what the best party would be this year. I had recommended bowling," he said with a chuckle.

Mom sat next to Dad and I stood off to the side, unsure where my place was.

"Now that you're all here, I suppose I should tell you why I'm here," Dr. Parker said. "I'm afraid I'm not just here to plan birthday parties." He paused for a moment looking around the room. I would soon learn that Dr. Parker always paused. I guess he had learned over the years that what he had to say was not easy to hear, and pauses increased what his patients retained from nearly nothing to slightly above that. "I'm with the oncology team. I'm here because something has come up on Sammy's blood tests that will need to be investigated further."

"What's oncology?" I asked looking around the room. Mom and Dad looked like they were going to pass out.

"Cancer," he replied.

CHAPTER 18

There were many words said in the hospital that day that I didn't understand—cancer was not one of them. My grandpa had died of lung cancer just before Sammy was born. Dad had told us it was because he smoked. Back in London, I'd had a friend whose mom had cancer in her back, or something like that, and she had also died. Cancer seemed to be everywhere. Everywhere adults were, that is. Not kids. I had never heard of kids getting cancer.

It had to be a mistake.

Our doctor had thought it was mono, what happened to that idea?

Mom must have been thinking the same thing. "How sure are you that this is...cancer?" she asked.

Dr. Parker sighed and pushed his round glasses up his nose. "We can't be sure until we've done a bone marrow biopsy, but at this point, I'm fairly certain. Sammy's blood cells are all low, which explains why he's been tired, out of breath and bruised, but we also saw something called a blast cell, which normally is only in the bone marrow. When we see it in the blood, it makes us think there might be something wrong. It makes us concerned about leukemia."

Leukemia? Blast cells? Bone marrow bio...or whatever he'd called it. Dr. Parker seemed to be speaking in a different language.

"What's that thing you said?" I asked.

Dr. Parker turned to me with a sympathetic look on his face. "What was what thing?"

"The bone thing."

He nodded. "The bone marrow biopsy."

"Yeah."

"We'll need to look at the cells inside Sammy's bones. In order to do that, we put a needle into his hip bone and pull off some of the cells from inside. Then we look at those cells under a microscope to see if there is any cancer there."

Hold on. Back up.

Did he just say a needle into the bone?! The room began to spin like I'd just put my head on a baseball bat and run in a circle. I felt like if I didn't sit I was going to fall over so I bent my legs and let myself slide to the floor. I could actually feel the blood drain from my face. My list of Worst Things Imaginable had just gotten one longer but for Sammy's sake, I decided to keep that to myself.

I looked at my brother. He was sitting silently in the bed watching us as if we weren't talking about him.

Was he not listening? Did he not hear Dr. Parker speaking as if he were narrating the latest volume in the *Goosebumps* series starring none other than Sammy himself? Six-year-old boy about to get a needle stuck into his bone and yet, six-year-old boy is mindlessly staring with nothing more than a blank look on his face. Wake up, six-year-old boy! Tell them this has to be a mistake! Tell them you feel fine or that you were just faking it. Why are you just sitting there as if you're watching cartoons or something? Why are you always too young to understand things that matter?

I wanted to go over and shake Sammy but I couldn't get up. There was a sick feeling in my stomach.

Dr. Parker was looking at me worriedly.

I looked over at Mom and Dad but I couldn't tell what they were thinking. Normally I could always tell exactly what they were thinking—Mom's are-you-hurt-face, Dad's I'm-concentrating-on-my-paper face, or both of their stop-teasing-your-brother-face—but right then they were as unreadable as a piece of white paper.

Dr. Parker walked over and offered his hand. I reached up and grabbed it and he guided me to Sammy's bed where I sat down by my brother's feet. The bed was way too long for Sammy; his feet barely went halfway to the end.

"Don't worry, it won't hurt," Dr. Parker said. "We'll give Sammy medicine to put him to sleep."

He kept looking at me so I felt obliged to nod though, really, that didn't sound much better. I pictured Sammy waking up to find someone standing over him with a white coat, giant needle and a crooked smile. Shhh, go back to sleep, the imaginary doctor whispered, this won't hurt...much.

Crust, I needed to stop reading *Goosebumps* books.

There was a long, uncomfortable pause where no one said anything. Dr. Parker walked over to Sammy and patted him on the knee. "Any questions from you, young man?" he asked.

Sammy looked over at me for a second then back to Dr. Parker.

"Will Cal get cancer too?" he asked.

"No," Dr. Parker said. "It's very unlikely."

"But we used the same spoon yesterday," Sammy said, a guilty look on his face.

Dr. Parker smiled. "You don't have to worry about that. It's not like a cold. You can't give it to someone by using the same spoon."

Sammy laid his head back on the pillow, but I could tell he was still thinking this through. I knew I'd have to explain everything later because I could tell when he didn't understand something. It was like when we'd be sitting in the tree fort reading a *Goosebumps* book and I'd read a word that he didn't understand. He'd let me read on a little further, but I knew he was still thinking about it because he always got this scrunched up look on his face when he didn't get something. Then a few sentences later he'd stop me and ask what "gruesome" meant, or whatever the word had been, and I'd have to stop and explain it to him.

"Any other questions?" Dr. Parker asked.

He looked first at Mom and Dad but their faces were still blank paper, then back to me.

Of course I had questions—lots of them. But more than anything I just had to ask, "Is Sammy going to die?"

The silence that overtook the room was terrifying. I saw Dad swallow hard and his eyes glaze over, Mom looked away as if I had just said the most awful thing imaginable. Dr. Parker's smile faded briefly but returned again—like the sun dipping behind a cloud before popping out the other side.

"Let's take things one step at a time. Right now, you don't have to worry about that. Once we do the bone marrow biopsy and have a better idea of what's going on, we'll know what medicines we can give Sammy to make him better. Sound like a plan?"

Why couldn't he have just said "no?" I'd wished so badly back then that he could have just said "no." One word would have meant the world to me. But I know now that he couldn't. He didn't know the answer. No one knew.

I spent the rest of that night thinking about the bone needle and whether Sammy was going to die while pretending to Sammy that I wasn't thinking about the bone needle and whether he was going to die.

After Dr. Parker had left, Mom and Dad stood up and said they needed to go grab something from the cafeteria. I could tell by the shakiness in their voices that they didn't need to go to the cafeteria, they just needed to go somewhere else. So they both hugged Sammy for a really long time and told him everything would be okay, even though they didn't know that everything would be okay, and just as Dad pulled away from Sammy he broke down and started to cry but instead pretended to be coughing, which only made it worse.

So Sammy and I were left in the room alone together and I suggested Crazy Eights to pass the time. I needed something to do so I could avoid the questioning look he kept giving me. I knew he was waiting for me to explain everything. He expected me to just drop my cards and say: "Look, Sammy, here's what's wrong and here's what's going to happen and here's what we're going to do." But I couldn't. This wasn't a question about a word in a book or how to make a fishing rod from sticks and string. It was over my head. And maybe I should have just told him that but I didn't. I'd spent my whole life being Sammy's know-it-all brother. Heck, I'd climbed the ranks to Eagle Level before he was even born. How could I just throw that all away? Instead, I just kept my head down and avoided Sammy's eyes, while a hole opened up inside me and a hollow feeling filled me up as if a shadow had crawled through my belly button and eaten my insides.

Dad and I drove home later that night as the sky grew dark. The country had never felt so lonely.

"Dad, do you think Sammy will be okay?" I asked at one point.

There was a long void that followed where only the tiny hissing noise of the wind outside the car window could be heard, and in that void I knew that Dad didn't think everything would be okay.

"I think so," he said, but his voice sounded funny, like he were talking through a fan.

"If Sammy dies, will he go to the same place as Grandpa? Or is there a separate heaven for kids?"

"He'd be with grandpa," Dad said, wiping his nose on his sleeve.

"Will Sammy be able to..."

Dad cut me off with a hand on my knee. "Try not to worry, Cal. Just try not to worry, okay?"

He was really telling me to stop talking, so I sat the rest of the way home quietly watching the dark, empty fields passing by and the occasional dark, empty farmhouse scattered between.

That night when I crawled into my bunk bed alone I couldn't fall asleep. I just lay with my eyes open watching the moonlight through the window cast wavy shadows like spiderwebs on the ceiling as it passed through Sakura and Big Tree outside. I had taken the quilt off the window; I wanted to be awake early. I closed my eyes to fall asleep but every time I did a new image formed behind my eyelids, forcing me to open them again. Sometimes it was Sammy playing basketball alone in the driveway, other times it was

Sammy kneeling in the driveway with a jar in his hands, and other times it was Mom and Dad, their chastising glares, their sad head shakes, and worst of all, their paper faces fighting to hide their tears in the hospital.

Chapter 19

The next day Mom called to say Sammy's bone needle wouldn't be happening until the afternoon, so I should go to school for the morning but Dad would pick me up after lunch.

Tom wasn't in class, I figured he'd been suspended or something. At least I didn't have to deal with him, but the other kids at recess continued to stare so Aleta and I found a quiet corner behind the grade four portable and sat down. It was nice—no one but us. No looks, no questions, which I suppose was fine with Aleta since she had been avoiding all the girls that kept asking her to join them and all the boys that had been ogling her from afar.

"So what did the doctors say?" Aleta asked when we sat down.

I debated how to answer. Should I tell her about Dr. Parker? Should I tell her what he'd said about Sammy maybe having cancer? It wasn't official until after the bone needle but it was still eating me up inside. Aleta was the only person I felt comfortable talking to, so I figured I might as well see what she thought.

"They think Sammy might have cancer," I said, choking a bit on the last word.

I didn't look to see Aleta's expression but I felt her back stiffen against the portable. "What?" she whispered. "Cancer? They think Sammy has cancer?"

I nodded. "That's what they said." I felt strangely distant from what I was saying. "We find out today when Sammy gets a needle into his bone to see if there's any cancer there."

Aleta didn't say anything for a really, really long time and we went back to the familiar silence we'd spent so many hours in over the summer.

"Well, maybe they're wrong?" she finally said. "If they're doing another test then they obviously don't have an answer. So maybe they're wrong about the cancer."

"Dr. Parker said he was pretty sure it was cancer."

"Pretty sure doesn't mean for sure," she said, "and besides they're always such downers there. They're all miserable and eager to give bad news. I'm sure they try to err on the side of caution just in case it is cancer."

"Huh?" I said, turning to Aleta. "What do you know about the hospital and what they're like?"

Aleta suddenly recoiled as if I'd caught her stealing one of Sammy's cookies off the cookie sheet. She looked away quickly. "Nothing," she said, but her hand instinctively went to her arm the way it often did when she was thinking about what made her sad. I could see the faint lines as she rubbed them.

"You were in the hospital, weren't you?"

She didn't say anything. I thought about pressing but I didn't. It was instinctive now. As soon as Aleta started rubbing her arm or she got the look on her face that told me I was treading close to the subject she didn't want to talk about, I backed off.

So we sat there for a while longer until the bell rang and it was time to go. I felt a sudden wave of fear rise up in me as we walked across the playground. I could see Dad's car waiting in the parking lot. I realized how nervous I was about Sammy's bone needle—and I wasn't even the one getting the needle.

"I wish you could come with me to the hospital," I said.

Aleta nodded but the rest of her body language said she wasn't keen on the idea. I thought about how much calmer I felt when she was around—how she'd helped me calm down when I was ready to punch Tom and Joey. It would be nice to have her there.

"If Sammy ends up staying over the weekend maybe you could ask your sister to drop you off for a visit."

Aleta stopped walking and looked at me. Her eyes looked pained and I wasn't sure if it was for Sammy or for something else. "I...I don't think I could ever go back there."

So she had been there.

I was going to ask her more but I saw Dad standing in the parking lot waving so I hurried across to meet him.

WHEN WE ARRIVED at the hospital Mom was sitting in the chair next to Sammy's bed while he slept. She put her finger in front of her mouth to shush us as we came in. The TV was on and Darkwing Duck was playing mutely in the background.

Next to Sammy's bed there was a plastic tray on the table and I lifted the cover to find a soggy piece of pizza next to a carton of milk.

"You can have that if you want," I heard Sammy say from the bed.

I looked up to find Sammy watching me. "No, thanks," I said, covering it back up and trying my best to hide the disgusted look on my face.

Dad walked over and sat on the end of his bed. "How are you feeling, sport?" he asked.

"Okay," Sammy replied, but he didn't look up at Dad. His lips were held tightly together and creases were splayed across his forehead.

"You're worried about the bone needle, huh?" Dad asked.

Sammy nodded.

If I were in his shoes I would have already bolted from the hospital but despite this I tried to reassure him.

"It'll be all right, Sammy. You're going to be asleep so it won't hurt."

"But what if I wake up?" he asked.

"You won't. Don't worry about that," Dad said, grabbing Sammy's foot and giving it a squeeze. "I've been put to sleep before, it was actually kind of fun."

"Fun?" Sammy and I replied in unison.

"Yeah, they tell you to count back from ten and say that you'll be asleep before you get to one. I don't even think I made it to eight," Dad chuckled. "Next thing I knew I was awake in the recovery room with all the ice cream I could eat."

"That doesn't sound too bad at all," I said, forcing a smile.

Sammy wasn't so easily convinced.

When Mom and Dad left to get coffee I took my chance to execute a plan I'd come up with while I'd lay awake the night before. If eating worms and walking through rose bushes were deserving of Levels, having a needle stuck into your bone sure as heck was too. I'd brought the journal with me to school in my backpack.

"I was going to give this to you after you'd finished," I said, pulling the journal out, "but I guess I could give it to you now. Sammy,

I award you the Level of Tiger—for bravery."

Sammy's eyes lit up the way they had so many times before. That simple leather-bound book with poorly illustrated animals could make my brother happier than anything.

"Tiger?! You mean it?" he asked.

I nodded.

For the rest of the afternoon I sat reading R.L. Stine's classic *Say Cheese and Die!* out loud to Sammy but I didn't use my scary voice. I was done trying to scare Sammy. There were real things to worry about now.

Later, two nurses came and said it was time. They unhitched Sammy's bed wheels and began manoeuvering him out of the room. I'd expected him to cry, or to protest, but instead he just lifted his hands beside his face, bent his fingers, and said, "Rawr," with a stubborn smile on his face.

CHAPTER 20

I SAT IN THE ROOM THE FOLLOWING DAY WATCHING DR. PARKER'S white moustache move up and down as his lips formed words that passed through my head like a breeze through an open window.

I guess I'd already known. But when he'd said he was pretty sure that Sammy had cancer the day before, a part of me had pretended it was like when I told my parents I was pretty sure I'd done my homework.

Acute Myeloid Leukemia, AML for short, is a form of blood cancer. It is caused by one cell, one tiny, insignificant cell saying, "I don't want to be like the rest." Then that one cell starts dividing and building an army. That army attacks the rest of the body and slowly takes over. It moves from the blood to the lungs to the liver and sometimes, it moves to the brain. Cancer has no boundaries. It doesn't care about anyone else, it just moves right on in and says, "Get out." Cancer is selfish.

At least, that's how Dr. Parker explained it.

The bone marrow biopsy had confirmed any parent's, brother's, sister's, grandparent's, or friend's worst nightmare—Sammy had cancer. And worse, Dr. Parker suspected that given the seizure it had already spread to his brain.

I felt like I was underwater. Like even though Dr. Parker was in the room, he was suddenly distant and hard to hear. I wanted to know what Sammy was thinking but when I looked at him he was just playing with a loose thread in his hospital sheets.

Nothing, Sammy wasn't thinking anything. I would have to think for him.

Dad sat on the bed next to Mom trying to conceal his sobbing while she asked every question an anxious mother could think of. What was the treatment? When did it start? What were the side effects? When would we know if it was working? And on, and on, and on...

Dr. Parker answered each question patiently. It was hard to be hysterical around someone with such a gentle voice. He was honest, which meant he never reassured, but all the while something in his tone and the way he sat with his hands folded gently in his lap, leaning in so we could hear him clearly, pausing frequently to let us think, made me feel that it just might be okay.

I tried to remember everything Dr. Parker said so that if Sammy asked me about it later I could explain it to him; but even with the pauses I couldn't keep up. Every other word seemed foreign and all the while I felt like I was in French class attempting to understand verb conjugations while someone sat under the table hammering a nail into my foot.

What I did manage to pick up went something like this:

Mom: "Is it curable?"

Dr. Parker: "Without spreading to the brain, AML is curable in about 50% of children." Pause. "With brain involvement, it is closer to 20%." Pause. "We will do everything we can to make Sammy one of those 20%, but it will not be an easy road."

Dad: Curses under his breath then apologizes.

Dr. Parker: "Don't apologize. It's how you should feel. I've been doing this job for over thirty years and I still feel that way every time I have to break bad news. I'd like to sit here and tell you it is going to be okay. That it's an easy road. But it isn't. The medicines Sammy will need are toxic to his body. He will be tired. He will be sick. His mouth will develop sores and his hair will fall out. He will need the support of his family more than ever. But we are going into this thinking Sammy will get better. If he responds to the treatment there is a possibility that he not only gets over this, but that he will be cured. Let's believe that that will be the case."

I heard what Dr. Parker was saying—be positive. Focus on the good. No point worrying about the worst-case scenario. And I wanted to. I wanted to think that someday Sammy would grow up to learn to read and climb and do all the other things six-year-olds don't know how to do. But it was hard. Sammy was never lucky with anything.

I looked at my little brother—pale, tired, skinny. I couldn't bear it like he seemed to. He'd spent months tired and bruised and sweating and losing weight and out of breath. He had endured it all and never once complained. Worse, he had endured it all while I had spent the summer avoiding him. Maybe if I'd been around I would have noticed. Maybe there would have been something I could have done. Maybe we could have caught the cancer before it had taken over his body. Maybe—just maybe.

"We will need to start treatment as soon as possible. You will be transferred to a room on the oncology floor and tomorrow we will start Sammy's chemotherapy," Dr. Parker said.

"And how long before we know if it's working?" Mom asked.

"Twenty-seven days. We will repeat his bone marrow biopsy in twenty-seven days and if we don't see any cancer cells in there it means we have induced remission. If we can induce remission the results are almost always favourable."

"And if we can't?" I heard the negative side of me say.

"If we can't, well, let's cross that bridge then."

Dr. Parker's face told me it was a bridge we didn't want to cross—not in twenty-seven days, not ever.

CHAPTER 21

THE NEXT MORNING WE WERE TRANSFERRED TO THE ONCOLOGY floor. It was a weekend so I didn't have school, which meant I could come early to the hospital with Dad.

I'd imagined the oncology floor differently; a place dedicated to children with cancer naturally conjures an image of gloom and fear and pity. I'd imagined a place of absent hair matching absent smiles, cries and moans haunting dark halls and darker rooms. To tell the truth, I was afraid of the oncology floor before I saw it, but when the doors opened and I saw the unit for the first time, my fears vanished.

If the rest of the hospital were a playground, the oncology floor was the giant slide in the middle. Paint splashed the walls and doorways in every variety. The wide hallways were well lit and voices—not cries—echoed from the nursing station in the middle. The unit, I would learn, was the shape of a bicycle wheel. Spokes of hallways spread from a central nursing station, each with rooms along them and a kitchen or a library or a games room at the end. We were directed to Room 18 halfway down one of those hallways. We were lucky—it was the hallway with the games room at the end.

For the first part of the morning Sammy and I sat on the bed playing cards while Mom set up the place as if we were moving in. The room was much the same as the one before: a hospital bed for Sammy, another bed pushed up against the window for Mom or Dad, a TV hanging on the wall and the now familiar tubes and wires and thingamabobbers all hospital rooms seemed to have. This room, however, had a third bed. A small cot was pushed right up against Sammy's bed and I smiled because I knew it was for me. The walls were white and near the top was a line of blue wallpaper with different animals repeating themselves around the room. A half-opened doorway in the corner revealed a bathroom and through the window I could see the early morning sun bathing an empty playground outside.

On the sill by the window Mom put up old pictures from home. One was taken outside our house in London with me in horrendous yellow overalls pointing proudly at Mom and Dad while they held a brand new baby bundled in their arms. Another was from only the year before—Sammy and I kneeling with our arms around each other by the river behind our house with makeshift fishing rods of sticks and string in our hands and goofy grins on our faces. It was scary to see the contrast between Sammy from the picture and Sammy lying in the hospital bed. Had I not seen him every day in between, I don't know if I would've recognized the two kids as the same. His skin was pink back then, not an off-shade of white, he was plump not skinny, and I realized that the dark circles under his eyes that I'd become so accustomed to hadn't always been there.

While Mom continued decorating in hopes that we might forget where we were, a nurse in Minnie Mouse scrubs came in and began doing the usual things nurses do. She counted Sammy's breathing, listened to his heartbeat, took his blood pressure (the black band around his arm—I was learning quickly), then told us she would be back with Sammy's chemotherapy. I remembered Dr. Parker describing chemotherapy as toxic. So when she returned with a bag full of yellowish-brown liquid and hung it on a pole next to Sammy's bed and attached it to the IV in his arm, a chill passed from the back of my neck down to my legs.

We sat playing cards on the bed but I kept getting distracted by the medicine dripping slowly from the bag into the tubing—drip, drip, drip. It was like when I sat in the bath and the tap kept dripping water even after the faucet was turned off—drip, drip, drip.

Sammy didn't seem to notice. He was concentrating hard on getting his cards right and he probably hadn't even heard when Dr. Parker said the medicines were toxic. Or more likely, he didn't know what toxic meant. I was so distracted I didn't even cheat or notice when Sammy won.

He looked up at me with a hesitant look on his face as he played his last card, waiting for the usual moment where I said something like, "Nope, you can't play that because the five of diamonds can never be the last card," then make him pick up five for "trying to cheat."

This time I only smiled and told him good job. He was utterly shocked and looked over at Mom by the window to see if she'd witnessed his victory. She hadn't, she was too busy reading *Childhood Cancer—A Guide for Family, Friends and Caregivers*.

"You want to play again?" I asked.

Sammy nodded but as we played the second game his face started to change. He looked tired all of a sudden and nearly as pale as the first day we'd come to the hospital after his seizure. He kept having weird twitches in his body and I thought he was hiccupping until one moment I was looking down at my cards and the next I was covered in vomit. Disgusting, slimy, yellow vomit. I looked up at Sammy and to be honest, my first reaction wasn't, "Are you okay?" but, "What the heck did you do that for!" until I saw that he was crying and holding his stomach.

Mom rushed over, grabbed Sammy, and tried to take him into the bathroom except he was still attached to his IV and she had to figure out how to unplug the pole from the wall. By the time they made it to the bathroom Sammy had thrown up again on the floor. I heard him heave a third time followed by something splashing in the toilet.

I was still covered in vomit and the smell was awful so I joined them in the bathroom and began scraping the barf off my clothes with paper towel and running my arms under the tap.

"I'm sorry, Cal," Sammy said, his head still in the toilet while Mom squatted next to him rubbing his back. "I'm really sorry."

He kept apologizing over and over between gags and heaves.

The nurse came in and cleaned up the bed and the floor. She gave me a matching hospital gown to Sammy's and said she could have my clothes washed. When Sammy came out of the bathroom he continued to apologize over and over, no matter how many times I said it was fine. I had to tell him to stop or I'd really be mad.

The rest of the morning I lay in my cot listening to Sammy rotate between retching and sleeping while I read *Cuckoo Clock of Doom*. I thought he'd eventually run out of stuff in his stomach and the God-awful noise of him puking would end, but even when there was nothing left the noises kept coming.

When I'd had enough of listening to Sammy puke I asked Mom if I could go to the games room. She didn't answer because she was busy holding Sammy's head up from the toilet so I took that as a yes and left.

CHAPTER 22

THE GAMES ROOM WAS ONLY TWO DOORS DOWN FROM OURS AND as I passed the one room in between I quickly glanced in. It was the same as ours only the kid who stayed there obviously had been there a lot longer. The whole room was covered with posters of hockey players, handwritten letters wishing someone named Oliver to get better and piles of toys beyond anything a normal kid should own. The bed was empty but by the window sat a woman dressed in a long black dress with white polka dots and a funny hat made of the same material. She looked like she was from some sort of old-fashioned movie and for some reason her outfit seemed vaguely familiar. She was rocking gently in a chair with her hands folded neatly in her lap staring out the window. She didn't look at me but I could see her face from the side and it looked like the face of someone who'd just watched their dog get run over by a car. The word sad just didn't seem to cut it.

I quickly hurried past, aware that I was being nosy, and entered the games room. At first it felt like I was dreaming. It was like someone had given me the key to Toys R Us and let me walk in alone. The walls were lined with shelves bowing under the weight of all the games and books and toys. There was an air hockey table, a foosball table and in the corner, a TV with every video game system I could name.

Now you'd think a room like that in a building full of children would be busier than a mall at Christmas but it was dead empty. There was only one other kid in the room and he sat in the chair by the TV with the top of his pale, bald head showing.

I walked around the room looking at the walls of board games and books, searching for any *Goosebumps* but finding none, before grabbing the air hockey puck and knocking it around the table a few times. I quickly realized that the room was going to be a lot more fun when I had Sammy with me. I thought about going back and seeing if he felt well enough to come but knew it would be a wasted trip so I instead kept wandering aimlessly around, lifting things off the shelves and putting them back again.

As I continued to look around I became aware that the boy by the TV had paused his game and was now looking over the chair at me. He was as skinny as a skeleton and as pale as snow. He reminded me of a birch tree with two tiny branches. His head was completely devoid of any hair and I'm not just talking about the top; eyebrows, eyelashes—everything was gone. His eyes were the palest blue I'd ever seen and he kept on staring at me without saying a word.

Finally, when I'd had enough of the awkwardness of being watched and couldn't find any game worth playing alone, I started walking toward the door to leave.

"You're the brother of the new kid, right?" the boy said with a funny accent I'd never heard before.

I stopped and turned toward him. "Yeah."

"Sammy, right? Sammy Sinclair. I saw it on the board at the front. What's your name?"

"Cal."

He motioned me to come sit in the empty chair next to him by the TV and since I wasn't really keen on going back to the barf room I went and sat.

"I'm Oliver," he said, turning back around to his game and unpausing it. "You know how to play Super Mario?"

I nodded. I'd had a few friends back in London with Nintendos but I'd never really played enough to be any good. So when he handed me the second controller so that I could try to guide Mario's sidekick, Luigi, over the giant crevasses in the ground it was a quick death.

Oliver didn't seem to mind. He took his turn and easily beat the level, reaching the end and jumping on a flagpole in a dramatic fashion that set fireworks off overhead, signalling his victory. His face showed no excitement, he just turned to me and said it was my turn as if nothing had happened.

We sat like that for a while, rotating turns—me quickly dying, him quickly beating each level before he started up the conversation again.

"So what's your brother's diagnosis?" he asked during one of his turns, apparently not really needing much concentration to play.

"Diagnosis?" I asked.

"Yeah, like what kind of cancer does he have?"

"Oh. Umm..." I had to think for a second. I'd heard the letters more than a few times in the last twenty-four hours but they still weren't sticking. "AM something," I said.

"AML," he said with a nod. "Not the best, but not the worst either. I've seen plenty of kids come through here with that."

"You have?" I said, not able to hide my surprise.

"Oh, sure. When you've spent 657 days in a hospital you've seen it all."

My mouth dropped. I wanted to think I'd misheard him but it had been so clear—657 days—and there was no hint of a smile or joke on his face. It was almost impossible to imagine.

Oliver noticed my surprise and smiled. "Don't worry," he said, "no one else has been here this long. Most kids are either cured or dead well before 657 days."

I felt a ball rise up in my throat when he mentioned the word dead but I did my best to ignore it. "So what's your...diagnosis?" I asked.

"My diagnosis? Failure to die." He laughed but when he saw that I didn't understand he continued. "They say I have 'undifferentiated carcinoma of the liver' but all that really means is that they have no idea. Some sort of cancer has made a home in my liver and no matter what kind of poisons the doctors tried to feed it, it didn't go away."

"So you've been getting chemotherapy for more than 600 days?"

"Oh, gosh no, are you kidding me? You think I'd let them do that to me? That'd be pure torture, man—pure torture. I'm well done with chemotherapy. Now I'm just waiting around for a miracle or death."

Listening to Oliver talking so easily about dying was unnerving. I'd never heard anyone, anywhere, talk about death so easily—not even an adult. And this boy was probably only twelve or thirteen at most. I realized that despite my fascination with *Goosebumps* books I had a real aversion to the topic of death.

"I've actually been home a few times but I keep having to come back because I can't eat without this," he said, lifting up his shirt to reveal a plastic tube coming out of his stomach, "and this," he said, pointing to the IV pole standing next to him. "Without any IV medications for my nausea I can't keep anything down."

I just sat there quietly taking my turns on the Nintendo because I didn't really know what to say.

"So your brother started his chemo today?" he asked.

I nodded.

"Started to get the chucks then, I bet?"

"The chucks?"

"Yeah, you know, vomit, puke, hurl, whatever you want to call it. We call it the chucks around here—or at least I do."

"Oh. Yeah, he's been throwing up all morning," I said.

He nodded knowingly. "Don't worry, he'll feel fine tonight. The first cycle isn't so bad."

I felt a little relieved.

"It gets progressively worse with each cycle. Just wait for the next two."

That was it. I'd had enough. I stood up quickly. "Sammy is probably wondering where I am," I said.

He seemed disappointed. "Okay, I'm sure I'll see you around. Come to Bingo night tomorrow—it's the best night around this place. And make sure you bring your brother—don't let him tell you he's too tired."

I nodded and started to leave, only stopping quickly at one of the shelves on my way out to grab a book.

I walked back down the hall to our room but stopped outside the door when I heard Mom and Sammy talking—Sammy sounded upset.

"But I know he is with her, Mom! I know he is!"

"Sammy, I promise you he's not with Aleta, he's just down the hall in the games room. If you let me run next door I can grab him and show you."

"Nooo," he cried, "don't leave too."

"Okay, okay, but I'm telling you, he'll be back soon. Don't worry."

There was a long silence and I gathered myself to make my entrance when Sammy continued.

"Mom, do you think Cal still likes me?"

"Why would you ask something like that? Of course I do."

There was no answer.

"Oh, Sammy, don't worry. Your brother loves you very, very much. He's just...well, he made a new friend this summer. That's all. But that doesn't change how he feels about you."

"But he doesn't want me around anymore. He only wants Aleta. Aleta is better at riding bikes, that's why. We went for a bike ride but I was too slow. And then he didn't want me around anymore."

I heard the bed creak and peeked in to see Mom hugging Sammy. He was crying into her shoulder.

I leaned back, my head resting on the wall, and closed my eyes.

Oh no, I thought, what have I done?

Sammy was right. I had completely ditched him over the summer for Aleta. Even the day before I'd been asking Aleta to come to the hospital with me. How could I have been so stupid and selfish? If I hadn't spent every minute of every day thinking about Aleta I would've noticed how sick Sammy was. It was like Aleta had cast some sort of spell over me and taken over my brain. I'd completely forgotten about my brother when I was with her and now look at him—he was sick with cancer and didn't even know if I liked him.

Well, I was going to change that. Right then and there I resolved to change that. I was going to be a better brother. I was going to stop thinking about Aleta and start thinking about Sammy.

I walked into the room and Sammy's face lit up. I went and sat beside him on the bed.

"Sorry, Sammy," I said, "I should have told you I was going to the games room." Mom looked at me crossly but I gave a knowing nod that I understood. "When you're feeling better we'll go to the games room together, okay? There are literally walls of toys and games and books and there's an air hockey table and a TV and video games and—"

Sammy heaved into the cardboard bowl the nurse had given him as a barf bucket. He definitely wasn't well enough for the games room.

"Maybe tomorrow we can go," I said.

"Okay," he said back, wiping his face and smiling.

I remembered the book in my hand that I'd grabbed from the games room—*The Secret Garden*. I'd had to read it in school and it was horrifically boring but I knew for certain it had no scary parts and wouldn't give Sammy nightmares.

"You want me to read this to you?" I asked, showing him the cover.

"What book is that?" he asked, his nose scrunching up as he tried to read the words.

"It's called *The Secret Garden*."

"Is it about monsters in a secret garden?"

"Nope."

"Vampires?"

"Nope."

Sammy paused, thinking. "Then what's it about?"

"A garden."

"Just a garden?"

"Yep."

He thought for a minute. "Is it good?"

"Not bad," I lied.

"Why can't we read *Cuckoo Clock of Doom*?" he asked, pointing to the book under my cot.

"I just thought it would be nice to read something different for a change."

Sammy looked really perplexed.

"But we always read *Goosebumps* books," he pressed.

"Yeah, I know. Which is why it might be good to try something new."

I opened the front cover and started to read, not giving him a chance to keep arguing.

He sat listening to me read the first few pages before his eyes began to flutter, then close. He was fast asleep before I'd even finished the first chapter.

I closed the book and put it under my bed then grabbed the copy of *Cuckoo Clock of Doom* and started reading. At least if Sammy had nightmares it wouldn't be because of me. It was my way of protecting him, or protecting myself, one of the two. It was my start to being a better brother.

CHAPTER 23

TRYING TO SLEEP IN A HOSPITAL IS LIKE TRYING TO FIND A FOUR-leaf clover with your eyes closed, which is ironic because Dad always said sleep was the best medicine. Needless to say, when Day Two rolled around, I was anything but keen to jump out of bed.

The sun lit our hospital room like it was hanging from the ceiling; I covered my head with my pillow. There was no quilt to block the morning sun. I was still half asleep when I heard Dr. Parker's voice.

"Good morning, boys. You awake in here? I've got something I want to show you."

Here's a little fact I learned in the hospital: doctors and nurses don't sleep. I pulled my head from under the pillow and looked at the clock—eight am.

Sammy was already awake and sitting up. "What is it?" he asked.

"It's my newest magic trick," Dr. Parker replied, turning on the light and pulling Sammy's bedside table to the centre of the room. He set three red cups upside down on it. "All right, can you both see?"

I sat up in my cot and nodded.

"Okay, what I've got here are three, perfectly normal, plastic cups." He lifted all three, one-by-one, showing us what looked like three very ordinary cups. "And what was underneath them, Sammy?"

Sammy looked confused. "Umm...nothing?"

"Correct. Except that if I take this magic wand from my pocket and tap each cup once, look what happens." He took a wand from his white coat pocket and tapped each cup lightly on top then returned the wand. As he lifted each cup again, a small red ball appeared underneath.

"Wow!" Sammy said, his eyes wide with disbelief as he looked over at me.

Dr. Parker replaced the cups over the red balls and continued, "Now, wouldn't it be great if we could make these red balls turn into something bigger, like basketballs?"

Sammy's eyes grew even wider. "Yeah!"

"I wish I could but I can't," Dr. Parker said with a smirk. "Basketballs wouldn't fit under these cups, now would they?"

"No," Sammy said with a frown, his eyes now returning to their regular size.

"I'm afraid that I'm stuck with these plain red balls," Dr. Parker said, faking disappointment as he lifted each cup again, this time revealing three baseballs.

Sammy let out a squeal. "They're...they're changed into baseballs!"

Dr. Parker looked down, then shot Sammy a look of surprise.

"So they are! Amazing! And here I thought I'd be stuck with those plain red balls forever." After a moment of inspecting the baseballs he looked back up. "And would you look at this! This one's signed by someone on the London Hurricanes. It says, 'To Sammy, Get Well, Mike Ribbon #23.'"

He tossed the ball onto Sammy's bed then grabbed the second

ball. "And this one is signed: 'To Cal, Help Him Through It, Mike Ribbon #23.'"

He tossed me the ball and I caught it.

"What about the last one?" Sammy asked.

"This one doesn't seem to have anything on it," he said, looking it over. "I guess I'll keep that one."

Dr. Parker put the cups and remaining baseball into his pocket and returned the table. "Since I'm here I might as well give you the once-over. Better make sure your head is still attached," Dr. Parker said, as he felt the front and back of Sammy's neck. The nurse had done the same thing the day before only she had said she was looking for knots or something like that. "And I'll make sure your heart is still beating." He pulled out his stethoscope and listened for a while over Sammy's chest. "Yep, good news, it's still beating. And lastly, I better make sure you have the right number of fingers." He took Sammy's hand and began counting. "One, two, three, four, six. Hmm, looks like you have too many. I guess we'll have to remove one. Let's see, which one is your least favourite?"

Sammy looked startled. "No! One, two, three, four, five!" he protested, counting each of his fingers for Dr. Parker to see.

"Are you sure?" Dr. Parker asked.

"Yes. Right, Cal?" Sammy said, turning to me.

I laughed. Sammy was so gullible. "Right."

"If you say so. I'll tell the nurses we don't need the finger clippers after all."

Sammy looked relieved.

Dr. Parker winked at me then walked over to the bed where Mom was sitting. She hadn't said a word.

"We'll be giving Sammy a different chemotherapy today."

"Is it dauna-something?" she asked.

"That's right—Daunarubicin. And then Etoposide tomorrow. After that, we'll wait a few days for his body to recover, then do it again."

"So that will be Cycle One?"

"Correct. We'll do three cycles—twenty-seven days in total. During the week we meet every morning with the rest of the oncology team and go through all your questions. Since it's a weekend you only get me. Any questions?"

Mom pulled out a piece of paper from her pocket on which she'd made a list. I can't say I remember what any of them were but Dr. Parker sat patiently beside her and answered them all.

Sammy and I were busy inspecting our new prizes. We didn't know who the London Hurricanes were but it didn't matter, a new baseball was a new baseball and we were both pretty excited.

Dr. Parker was still talking with Mom when Sammy's nurse came back in with an IV bag in hand. She hesitated when she saw Dr. Parker but he waved her in.

"How are you feeling today, Sammy?" she asked.

He shrugged. He was too interested in the ball to care so she went about doing her usual routine. She hung another bag on the IV pole—this one an orangey colour—then pushed a few buttons on the box that was attached lower down on the pole. "Okay, I'll be back to check on you periodically. If you need any help getting up to the loo, just push the call button on the side of your bed."

As Dr. Parker started to leave he turned one last time to Sammy and me. "Don't forget to go to Bingo night tonight—six pm in the games room. It's a favourite of the kids around here. Great prizes."

I nodded. I'd already intended to go after Oliver had mentioned it. I just hoped Sammy would be able to go too.

CHAPTER 24

SAMMY'S RETCHING STARTED SOONER THAT DAY. IT WAS LIKE A horrible metronome keeping track of the time. Minute, retch, minute, retch, minute until nothing more came out—just gags and groans and gargles.

When Dad showed up it was almost noon and Mom looked cross. "What took you so long getting here?"

The whites of his eyes were a bright red and for the first time in a while he hadn't shaved. Black bristle daubed with white covered his face. "Sorry," he said, then he sat on the end of Sammy's bed. "How ya' feeling, sport?"

Sammy answered with a heave.

I spent Day Two the same way I spent Day One—bored. Sammy rotated between heaving and sleeping while I watched TV or tried to get him to play Connect Four. I even offered to read him more of *The Secret Garden* but he said no, and since I wasn't really interested in the book either, I put it aside.

By mid afternoon Mom had softened a little toward Dad and they sat on their bed reading. Mom continuing her book on cancer, Dad rotating between different magazines from the library.

I spent a few hours playing video games in the games room, secretly hoping Oliver would show up but he never did. When I couldn't look at the words *Game Over* another time I returned to my cot and argued with the clock to hurry up. It was stubborn. The minute hand never slowed or sped up, it just trucked along at the same horribly slow pace.

"It's almost six o'clock," I announced at five forty-five. "You ready for Bingo night?"

Mom set down her book and looked at the clock. "I don't think Sammy feels up for Bingo night. He's had a rough day."

"I'm okay," Sammy lied as he suppressed another gag. "I feel fine."

Mom looked doubtful. "Are you sure?"

"Sure as sure," I said, answering for Sammy as I hopped out of my cot.

Sammy was less enthusiastic in his dismount but climbed from bed all the same. His hospital gown had come undone and Mom took a few minutes tying it back up. Outside the room I could already see a slow stream of children and parents moving toward the games room.

Dr. Parker was right. Bingo night was a floor favourite. It was run by a group of volunteers that looked like they were probably in high school wearing red vests with embroidered teddy bears on the front. The head of the volunteers was a girl named Marribeth; she had crooked teeth and a raspy voice. "You know the routine, everyone grab a card, a dabber and have a seat," she said smiling, only her croaky voice made her sound grumpy.

We sat at a table near the back and watched as more and more children entered.

"Cal," Sammy said, pulling on my sleeve as he watched a mother walk in with a little boy not much bigger than he was. "Why do they all look so weird?"

The boy looked no different than the rest of the kids on the floor—bald and skinny as a toothpick. "They have cancer," I said, leaning in close so no one would hear me.

"But why don't they have hair? I have cancer and I have hair."

Sammy looked genuinely frightened.

"I think that's from the medicine," I said.

"Will I lose my hair?" he asked, reaching up and touching his head as if to check that it was still there.

I wished Mom would stop talking to the lady at the table next to ours so she could rescue me from the conversation. I didn't want to lie but I didn't want Sammy to start crying either.

Thankfully, Oliver walked in at that moment, followed by his mother pushing his IV pole. She was still wearing the same polka dot outfit from the day before—or maybe she had a few of the same outfits. He walked straight up to our table. "You ready to win some prizes?" he asked, taking the empty seat on the other side of me. He looked over at Sammy and smiled.

"You're Sammy right? I'm Oliver."

Sammy nodded back but looked intimidated. He'd never been a shy kid before he'd gotten sick but something had changed in him since coming to the hospital. He wasn't the boisterous little brother who talked incessantly even when I wanted him to be quiet. He'd become a shy little kid who hardly talked when the nurses came in the room and never had questions despite people constantly asking him over and over again if he did. I'd thought initially it was because he was too weak but looking at Oliver, who was twice as frail as Sammy, I realized it must have been something different. In fact, looking around the room, all the kids looked frailer than Sammy—the room was full of gaunt, skeleton-like frames attached to tubes and IV poles.

Oliver must have noticed me staring around the room because he leaned in close, careful to speak quietly enough so that our moms couldn't hear.

"You looking at the little girl with Down Syndrome?" he asked.

I didn't know what Down Syndrome was but I had been staring at a little girl two tables over with small, oval shaped eyes and a tongue that didn't seem to fit in her mouth. She was already dabbing away at her Bingo card despite her mother trying to explain that she had to wait. It didn't seem to matter to her how the game was played—she was content just dabbing.

"Her name's Gracie. She's three years old and has ALL."

"ALL?" I asked.

"The nicer cousin of your brother's AML. 95% cure rate—the best odds of any cancer."

"Oh," I said, thinking this through in my head. Why couldn't Sammy have had that cancer? "And what about that girl in the wheelchair?" I said, pointing at another girl sitting across the room with a disinterested look on her face. She was the oldest in the room—well into her teens—and it seemed like she'd been dragged to Bingo night rather than come willingly. Like everyone else, she was bald and skinny with prominent bones sticking out of her cheeks and below her neck. Unlike the rest, she wore regular clothes instead of a faded blue hospital gown. I imagined she would have been pretty before she'd gotten sick.

"Jessica Walter, seventeen years old, osteosarcoma," Oliver said, without a hint of hesitation pronouncing the last word. "She used to be a big-time ballet dancer before she had her leg amputated."

"Amputated?" I said, lifting my bum off the seat a bit so I could get a better look. Sure enough, just like Oliver had said, she had one leg on the footrest of her wheelchair and where the other one should have been there was nothing.

"Yep, amputated. One day she came home from dance with a pain in her thigh but her mother told her it was a muscle cramp. So she went for massage therapy and saw a chiropractor and all the while kept dancing because that's what her mother wanted her to do. She told me that she never even liked to dance, she just kept doing it because she couldn't tell her mom she hated it.

"Well, finally, the pain got so bad she had to pull out of some big dance competition and her mom took her to the doctor. The X-ray showed that the cancer had literally eaten away most of her leg bone." Oliver made a horrendous chomping noise for effect. "Next thing, her leg was gone, she was getting chemotherapy and now has a ten percent chance of still being alive in five years."

I noticed the girl had a woman sitting next to her—most of the kids had their moms with them—and I couldn't help but feel like her mom had a remorseful look on her face. Probably it was just Oliver's story affecting me, but still, the distance between the daughter and mother was perceivable from across the room.

Bingo night was filling up quickly and there were only a few spots left at the tables. At the front, the volunteers looked to be getting ready to start but held off as the last few stragglers wandered in.

The last group was a man followed by a woman with a beautiful long dress. They had brown skin and the lady had one of those funny red dots between her eyes. Behind them came two boys holding hands. The older boy was guiding the smaller one into the room and it was obvious who the sick one was—the smaller boy had a shuffled gait and a yellow tube running from his face into his nose. They were both smiling and when they sat down at a table the older boy helped the younger one with his Bingo dabber. They reminded me of Sammy and me when we were younger.

Once again, Oliver followed my eyes across the room. "Hassan and his twin brother, Amir," Oliver said. "Hassan has metastatic neuroblastoma. At most, he'll live a few more months."

"Twins?" I replied.

Oliver nodded. "Proof that cancer kids don't grow like normal kids. Look at me, I'm sixteen and I look like I'm thirteen," Oliver said.

I was shocked but pretended not to be. I'd definitely thought he was twelve or thirteen.

While we sat and waited for the game to start Oliver continued to list off the various diagnoses around the room as if he were reading a shopping list. He seemed to know everything about cancer and everyone with cancer. I guess when you've lived in a hospital for as long as he had, you just sort of picked things up.

The game finally started and Marribeth croaked out number after number. The room hushed as everyone concentrated on their sheets to be sure they didn't miss a possible dab but Oliver didn't once look down at his Bingo card. As he continued talking I remembered back to his room full of toys and realized he'd been to more than a few Bingo nights. I guessed he no longer came for the prizes; it was more for the company. And I was quite happy to have the company too. Not because I lacked people to talk to, but I lacked knowledge. From Oliver I would get the answers to all the questions Sammy had. It would let me be what my brother expected—a guide.

"Bingo!" the first winner shouted. She was a little girl sitting sandwiched between her mother and father at the same table as the girl in the wheelchair. ALL, I recalled Oliver saying, she would probably be fine. Her face had instantaneously gone from a concentrated gloom to a full-faced smile. Even the wheelchair girl next to her was smiling.

Marribeth walked over and checked her card and after it was verified, the girl walked to the front of the room where a huge caravan covered with an assortment of plastic-wrapped toys and plush stuffed animals sat. She chose a green frog stuffy and hugged it close to her chest as she walked back to her mom and dad.

After that the atmosphere in the room changed. Anticipation, a low din of excitement, smiles and eager eyes—even Sammy looked a lot happier once he realized that there were tangible goods to be won.

Three Bingos later and it was my turn. I practically leapt from my chair as I screamed the word, "Bingo!" After Marribeth had agreed it was true, I raced to the toy caravan and began looking over all the goods. After a short while I settled on a Lego airplane that looked awesome but I would later learn was nearly impossible to put together.

As I walked back to the table I saw Sammy beaming with excitement for me. My heart sank a little. Sammy still hadn't won. Sammy and his darn luck.

With each passing Bingo it became more and more apparent

that Sammy wouldn't win. And then Marribeth announced that it would be the last game and one of the tiny kids who couldn't even play but whose parents played for him won. They carried the kid up to the cart and he grabbed the nearest stuffy because it was soft, not because he understood what it was. As they walked back toward their table the kid dropped the stuffy and probably wouldn't have noticed if they'd never picked it back up.

I felt sad for Sammy. More so, I felt angry with myself. I should have told him he could go up and choose something instead of taking the Lego airplane. I couldn't bear to look at him despite the fact that he was still smiling. My selfishness had reared up again and I hated it. I felt as if every person in the room were looking at me. "That's the boy who didn't let his brother get anything," they must be thinking. "And he's not even sick."

"Okay, that's the end of Bingo night," Marribeth croaked and I thought I saw Sammy sink a little in his chair. "Anyone who didn't win a prize may come up and choose one from the cart."

Sammy jumped from his chair, forgetting about the IV attached to his arm, and started toward the front. Mom barely had time to catch him with the pole before he tore it out. When he returned he had plastic-wrapped walkie-talkies.

"Awesome!" I said, looking at them. "I didn't see these!"

We had gotten a pair of walkie-talkies a few years back for Christmas but they were much smaller and barely worked from one end of the house to the other. These ones looked heavy duty. They were big and black with lots of buttons and knobs on them and the moment Sammy and I got back to the room we asked Dad to open them. While Sammy sat in his bed I proceeded to walk down the hospital corridor periodically asking, "Can you still hear me?"

In the end it turned out they worked further than the hospital would allow me to walk. Even at the cafeteria I could clearly make out what Sammy was saying, his crackly voice echoing, "robber that," after everything I said because I couldn't explain to him over the walkie-talkie that it was "roger" not "robber."

CHAPTER 25

THE WEEKEND WAS OVER AND I HAD TO GO BACK TO SCHOOL. I'D spent the night before in my own room, tucked into my own bed and in the morning brushed my teeth in my own bathroom and ate at my own kitchen table, and yet something about it all felt foreign and unfamiliar. Maybe it was that Sammy wasn't right next to me spilling his milk everywhere, or that Mom wasn't there telling me to stop being mean when I called him a pig, or that Dad slept in and I had to get myself ready for school.

When it was almost time to leave Dad walked down the stairs into the kitchen rubbing his eyes.

"Sorry, Cal, I must have slept through my alarm," he said.

"It's fine," I replied through a mouth full of Cheerios.

He sat down next to me at the table and for a moment looked as if he was going to say something. Instead he just stared blankly through me, as if I weren't there or he had x-ray vision, before grabbing an old newspaper and opening it. His beard had grown more and he had a hunch while he sat, like he'd become an old man overnight. It was sometime around then that I realized Dad was having the hardest time of all of us dealing with Sammy's cancer.

Outside the air was cool and the leaves were starting to show the changes of autumn. A hurried breeze blew through the grass around our house and it tickled my nose as it went. After summer, autumn was my favourite season. I liked the smell of damp leaves and the yellows and oranges and golds of the maples. When we'd lived in London we used to drive through the country just to see the trees and pumpkin patches. Then we'd stop somewhere and choose the biggest, orangest pumpkin we could possibly find. Now that we lived in the country, it was all around us. Only I'd never really appreciated it before.

When I saw the familiar yellow school bus kicking up a cloud of dirt down County Road 11 I felt a wave of anxiety pass through me. By now, every kid at school would know about Sammy's cancer. We hadn't gone to church the day before but I knew that Reverend Ramos would have asked everyone to say a prayer for Sammy, and then people would have talked at length over Sunday dinner about the sick boy who had collapsed on the playground and been diagnosed with cancer.

They'd probably have some sort of fundraiser at the church like they always did when something bad happened. Like when the Maxwell's farm flooded or the Granger's house caught fire, people were always willing to help if something bad happened to someone else. I remember wondering if I'd be able to get a new bike with the money—just for a second—but yeah, I actually had that thought.

An awkwardness followed me around everywhere that morning—the cautious smile from the bus driver, the stifled chatter as I took my seat, the hurt that filled Aleta's eyes as she sat silently beside me. Even the Riley brothers greeted me with little more than a sneer, though I doubted they were quiet out of respect. The bruises on the back of Tom's neck told me that fear had a role to play.

I wanted to scream. I wanted to smack the smugness off the Rileys' faces and scream. Come on! Have it out! Yes, it's me—the one whose brother has cancer! He's not dead you know! And I'm not him! Instead I sat quietly and stared out the window at the passing fields that had once been towering corn and green soy but now were empty and brown.

Nobody spoke to me the whole morning but when the bell rang for recess Ms. Draper asked me to stay behind.

She waited for everyone else to leave, then turned to me.

"How are you doing?" she asked.

It was a question I would get a lot.

I thought about saying, "Oh, you've mixed up the brothers. I'm actually the one that doesn't have cancer," but I didn't have it in me to be rude.

"Fine," I said.

I told her I was fine because I should have felt fine. I wasn't the one retching in a toilet. But in truth I didn't feel fine. I felt achy all over my body and tired like I hadn't slept in days.

"Are you sure you're okay?" Ms. Draper asked again.

"I'm fine," I repeated.

The main reason I said I was fine was that it was the quickest end to the conversation.

Ms. Draper nodded her head slowly. "Okay, but if you ever want to talk about things you know I'm available, right?"

I nodded.

Outside I'd expected to find a crowd but instead found only Aleta kicking at some stones by the portable door. She smiled at me hesitantly.

I didn't smile back.

Instead I started walking toward the far end of the playground.

Aleta followed beside me.

"I heard about Sammy," she said. "At church, Reverend Ramos made an announcement. I'm sorry, Cal." She sounded genuinely sorry. She sounded like she might start to cry, which irritated me because I blamed her for keeping me away from Sammy.

I walked faster.

Aleta walked faster to keep up.

"What did the doctors say? Will they be able to...make him better? Will he have to be in the hospital long?"

We walked past the boys playing basketball and the girls playing hopscotch. We walked right off the concrete that surrounded the school and were now crossing through the large field beyond. A few younger kids were playing tag but stopped to watch as we walked by. I kept walking, not paying attention. I walked until I was halfway across the field and stopped.

"Are your parents doing okay? My dad was wondering—"

I cut Aleta off with a wave of my hand. "Aleta, remember when you told me some things are easier to not talk about?"

Her green eyes flashed a moment of recollection.

"This is one of those times," I said with more anger in my voice than I'd meant. "I really don't want to talk about Sammy. I really don't want to talk about anything. I just want to be left alone."

"Cal, when I said—" she sounded like she was going to argue

then stopped. For a moment she stood there, her eyes locked on mine. She was searching me—trying to break me down. And she almost did. But I held strong—my face solid and fierce. I couldn't let her break me down. I couldn't let Sammy down again. Aleta let out a deflated exhale and looked back toward the school. "Okay," she said, "I understand."

"Thanks," I said gruffly, then turned and continued walking toward the far side of the schoolyard.

When I got to the chain-linked fence that separated the school from the farms and fields beyond I followed it until I was at the furthest point possible from the school. I turned and sat with my back against the cold metal, watching the kids play.

Aleta was still standing where I'd left her in the middle of the field. I was supposed to feel better. I had done what I had thought I needed to do—I had stood up for Sammy. I had put Sammy first. Yet, I didn't feel better.

My heart still ached. It ached for Sammy. It ached for Aleta. But I needed to stop worrying about Aleta. Aleta would be fine. Sure she didn't know anyone else at school and sure she was quiet as a mute, but she would make friends. She would find new people to play with. She would have to. I couldn't be her friend anymore.

CHAPTER 26

It was Friday, Day Eight. The first week was over and it had not been easy on anyone.

The day after I'd told Aleta I needed time alone I'd climbed on the bus and sat in the aisle seat, not moving over when she'd gotten on. For a moment she'd stood waiting, but then the bus had lurched forward, continuing down Thornton Road and she'd gone and sat a few seats behind. Throughout the morning I'd avoided her pleading eyes until the bell rang for recess. I'd rushed to be the first out the door and I walked straight to the end of the playground. Aleta hadn't followed. She'd stood around the portable for a while until one of the girls had come up to her and pulled her into their group. But even then she was still trying to put me in another of her trances. I could see her looking back at me every chance she got.

That first day had been the hardest—no doubt. After a whole summer with Aleta it felt like I wasn't just losing a friend—I felt like I was losing a part of my body. Like I was cutting my arm off or something. But I knew it had to be done. For Sammy's sake, it had to be done.

Dad picked me up fifteen minutes late that day—each day he took a little longer coming to get me from school. And each day he'd arrive with a little more hair on his face and a little less energy in his voice. Then we'd drive to the hospital with only a short "How was your day?" passing between us.

I was glad for the school week to be over. It meant I could sleep on the cot for the weekend and not have to worry about the kids at school teasing me, or getting myself ready in the morning without Mom's help, or having to look at Sammy's empty bunk when I climbed out of bed. Mostly, I was looking forward to having time with Sammy so I could make things right between us. Even after a whole week of trying I didn't seem to be making any headway. But the night before I'd come up with an idea that I was sure would work. I was going to right all the wrong I'd done that summer.

When we arrived at the hospital Mom was talking at the nurse's desk with a lady I recognized from Bingo night.

"Hi, honey," she said, giving me a quick wave from across the nursing station before turning back to the woman.

I waited beside Dad while he signed us in.

"Any cough, fever, or cold-like symptoms?" the nurse behind the counter asked. It was always the same questions. It reminded me of going through security at the airport except on the oncology ward your weapon is your germs.

We both shook our heads and held out our hands so she could place a dab of sanitizer into them.

When we walked around to the other side of the nursing station Mom was finishing her conversation. The woman she was talking to had red, shoulder-length hair and a pin on her shirt that read: *Parents Fundraiser Committee*. I was trying to remember who her child was when it hit me—Marsha! Her daughter's name was Marsha. She was eight years old and had brain cancer that they'd had to open her skull to take out. Oliver had told me this and his descriptions were never easy to forget.

"Eight o'clock in the big room next to the cafeteria," Mom said. "We'll be there."

She turned to Dad and me and we all walked back to Sammy's room.

"What's at eight o'clock?" Dad asked when we got to the room.

"The parents' volunteer meeting tonight," Mom said, "I told Barb we'd both come." Mom's tone sounded like it was a done deal but Dad's face didn't look very happy about that.

"Lizzy," Dad said, he always called Mom Lizzy when he wanted something, "I...I..."

"I, what?" Mom asked.

"I just don't think right now is the right time for me to start joining things. Why don't I stay with the boys—take them to the games room. You can go."

"Harold, please don't make this an argument. It would be nice to get involved around here—like it or not we're going to be here for a while—and it won't kill you to spend a couple hours a week giving back."

Dad's shoulders slumped. "Liz, I'm telling you—I'm not going. I'm sorry, but it's just not for me."

"But I've already told Barb we'd both—"

Dad held up his hand. "I'm not going, Liz."

Mom's face tightened into a scowl but she didn't keep arguing. Instead she went to her bed, sat down and picked up her latest book—*Surviving Childhood Cancer: A Guide For Families* and Dad walked over to Sammy's bed.

Sammy had been flipping through his baseball card binder, pretending not to listen.

"How's it going, sport?" Dad asked.

Sammy put the cards down. "Good."

"How's your tummy?" I asked, walking up to the bedside table. "Is it still hurting?"

His stomach had been bothering him all week even with the pain medicines the nurses gave him.

Sammy shrugged. "It's fine."

I reached inside my backpack and pulled out a piece of paper and pen. "Okay," I said. "How bad is your tummy pain?"

It was time to start implementing my plan but Sammy just looked at me with a confused expression.

See, I had been thinking it through the night before. Why didn't Sammy seem excited to hang out with me anymore? What had changed? Well, I knew it was the summer—yes—but I figured that couldn't be all of it because there were still times when we'd go to the games room and suddenly he'd be back to himself.

Then it came to me. It was what the doctors and nurses called his symptoms—his tummy pain, his nausea, his headaches. The nurses were always asking how bad his tummy pain was on a scale of zero to ten but they only came in every few hours unless we asked for them. My idea was to keep track of Sammy's symptoms so I could ask the nurses for more pain medicines when he needed them. That way his tummy wouldn't bother him so much and he'd want to spend more time in the games room with me.

I repeated my question, "How bad is your tummy pain right now?"

Sammy shrugged. "It hurts a bit."

"No, I mean, like, on the zero to ten scale the nurses use. Ten being the worst pain you've ever felt and zero being no pain." I said it just like the nurses always said it. "I'm going to start writing it down for you. That way when it gets bad I can ask the nurses to bring you more pain medicines."

Sammy didn't seem overly excited about this but Mom was looking over her book with a smile so I knew she must have liked the idea.

"Oh," Sammy said. "Six, I guess."

"Six," I repeated, then wrote the number six on the paper. Above it I wrote the date and time.

Six was almost always Sammy's answer when he hadn't got his pain medicines in a while. A seven was when his tummy was really bothering him and he'd only given an eight once when he was keeled over the toilet grabbing his tummy. That had looked more like a ten to me but Sammy wasn't very good with numbers so he'd given it an eight. After the pain medicines his pain would usually go down to a two or three or four, but never a zero.

"Okay, and do you have pain anywhere else?"

Sammy shook his head.

"Good." I wrote, 'No pain anywhere else' next to the six. "How many times have you thrown up today?"

Sammy thought for a minute then held up two fingers.

"And do you feel like you need to throw up right now?"

Sammy shook his head again.

"Okay," I said, scribbling more notes.

I finished up my report and was pretty happy with how it looked. Very official, I thought. Then I grabbed *The Secret Garden* from under my bed and held it up.

"Want me to read a chapter?" I asked.

Sammy looked at the book for a second then shrugged.

Good enough—I started to read.

After Mom left for her meeting, Dad took Sammy and me to the games room. We played air hockey for a while—taking turns against Dad—but then Sammy said he liked watching better. I could tell by the way he winced every time he leaned over to hit the puck that it was because of his tummy that he didn't want to play, not because he liked watching better. I guess Dad noticed too because he asked Sammy if he wanted to go back and lie down and Sammy didn't answer, which we both knew was a yes. So after only fifteen minutes in the games room we went back to our usual prison and I sat watching TV while the nurses came in and gave Sammy more pain medicines. Or maybe they were sleeping potions because within five minutes Sammy's breathing had become the regular, rhythmic in and out that meant he was asleep.

I thought about asking Dad if we could go back to the games room but I knew we couldn't leave Sammy alone. So I waited for Mom to come back from her meeting. But I guess it went late because when she arrived Dad stood up and said he needed to get home.

So I just watched TV, remembering back to the beginning of summer when I'd complained about not having a TV in Huxbury. Right then I would have been happy to never see another TV as long as I lived.

CHAPTER 27

It was Sunday morning and we were waiting for Dad. There was a chapel in the hospital and Mom wanted to go to Sunday service but Dad was late and Mom was angry. It didn't bother me—I'd rather have gone to the games room to see if Oliver was around, and it definitely didn't bother Sammy (he was half asleep on his bed watching cartoons). Still, I hoped Dad would show up soon because I could feel the tension in the room mounting every time Mom looked at the clock.

When Dad finally strolled in I braced for impact.

"How ya' feeling, sport?" he asked Sammy; his usual routine when he arrived.

Sammy said, "Fine."

Dad stood watching the TV for a brief moment. I think he was collecting his thoughts to prepare himself for Mom. He walked across the room and sat down beside her on the bed.

"It's 10:30, Harold," Mom said, her voice surprisingly calm.

Dad didn't say anything back.

"I wanted to go to the service this morning in the chapel. You had promised you'd be here by nine so we could go."

"I'm sorry, honey, I didn't get much sleep again and—"

Mom stood up and walked toward the door. She stopped for

a second and I thought, "Okay, here it comes," but then she just walked right out without saying a word.

I realized I'd been holding my breath and let it all out with a giant whoosh.

"Can we go to the games room?" I asked Dad optimistically.

Dad didn't answer. I think maybe Mom's guilt trip had turned him to stone.

On Monday I went back to school ready for another painful week of avoiding Aleta only to find out I wouldn't have to. When the bus pulled up in front of her house she wasn't there. We waited a few minutes before driving off and instead of feeling relieved like I should have, I felt sad.

By Thursday, Aleta still hadn't shown up for school and things still weren't any better with Sammy. Just like Oliver had said, Cycle 2 was worse than Cycle 1. He barely had the energy to get out of bed to go to the bathroom, let alone to go to the games room or do anything fun. He didn't want me to read to him, he didn't want me to get him a warm towel to put on his tummy, he just didn't seem to want me at all.

This was also around the time he started losing his hair.

I first noticed it when we were lying on his bed side-by-side watching TV. I thought he was asleep until I heard the baseball he'd had in his lap drop to the floor and he moved to try to reach it. I was going to get up and help him when I noticed something. At first I thought it was a dead animal—like he'd just killed a squirrel by sleeping on it—but then I realized Sammy's pillow was covered in his dark brown hair. I thought back to his reaction at Bingo night when he'd seen the other bald kids and I quickly flipped his pillow over before he turned back around. I thought I could hide it from him but later that night he'd gone to the bathroom and when he'd come back he'd seen his pillow. For a while he'd just stood at the side of the bed staring. He looked like he was going to cry. After needles and nausea and tummy pain—it was losing his hair that seemed to bother Sammy the most.

He'd reached up and touched the top of his head.

"You've still got lots left," I said, which I don't think was the right thing to say because in only a few short days he didn't.

By the fifteenth day of treatment, Sammy's tummy pain was getting so bad that he couldn't eat. When I asked Dr. Parker why, he told me it was because the army of cells the cancer was building was fast so the medicines he gave had to kill fast-multiplying cells. Unfortunately those medicines couldn't tell which cells were cancer and which were normal. So the normal cells that grew quickly—like mouth and stomach and hair—all got killed. That's why his hair was falling out and why he needed a feeding tube—a yellow straw that went in his nose like all the other kids had. It reminded me of a gas pump—except the tube put food into Sammy's tummy rather than gasoline.

When the next weekend started I wasn't feeling as optimistic as the one before. Either the hole I'd created during the summer was too big or Sammy's symptoms were too much for medicines to help—because nothing seemed to make him feel any better.

I came to a new conclusion—Sammy was depressed.

I'd heard of people being depressed from school. One of the kids had said they couldn't live with their dad anymore because he was depressed. I'd asked Mom what he'd meant and she'd said, "Depressed is when someone is so sad that they just don't feel like doing anything anymore."

And that was Sammy.

He was so sad he didn't feel like doing anything anymore.

He was sad about his cancer, he was sad about his hair, he was sad about his brother abandoning him, and lately, he was sad about how much Mom and Dad fought. Or at least, I was sad about that.

Before Sammy's cancer Mom and Dad never fought. Well—not never—but almost never. I can think of one or two times they had gotten into an argument about something before Dad had made a joke and Mom had laughed and they'd figured it out. Now that the jokes were over, there was no end to their arguing.

On that particular day it was about Dad reading magazines when Mom wanted him to start reading a cancer book she'd just finished.

"Don't you want to have some idea of what's going on around here?" Mom asked.

"I do. I listen to the doctors," Dad replied, over his magazine. "They've spent years reading books so we don't have to. If it makes you feel better to read up on the names of all the different medicines, go ahead. But that's not my way and I don't need you telling me what's the right way or the wrong way."

"It's not just about learning the names of the medicines, it's about having some idea of what's going on. It's about taking some interest in your son. You arrive here late, you leave here early—how do you think that makes Sammy feel?"

"Oh Christ, Liz," Dad said, throwing his magazine onto the bed next to him. "I'm trying, okay? I really am."

Their voices had started at a whisper but had grown louder as their argument went on.

Sammy was pretending to be asleep but I knew he was awake. I could always tell when he was awake.

"Maybe if you'd—" Mom started to say something else but I cut her off.

"Sammy's awake, you know," I said, and pointed at his bed. Sure enough the lump beneath the covers moved and a little head poked out.

"Sorry, Sammy," Mom said, looking really guilty. She walked over to his bed. "We didn't mean to wake you."

She cast a furious glance back at Dad.

"Yeah, sorry, sport," Dad said. "We'll try to keep our voices down."

"Because it would be really nice for once if we didn't have to listen to your fighting," I said sharply, standing up in an angry huff and walking to the door. "I'm going to the games room."

I don't think they heard. Or at least I don't think they cared. I had become a shadow on the wall. The healthy son who would still be there next year and the year after that. And I know it was selfish but I felt rejected. The basketball league Dad had promised was gone, school events of any kind weren't an option, and my parents had already cancelled our Thanksgiving trip to Vermont. Life outside the hospital had been put on hold and I couldn't help but feel upset.

Mom, Dad, me—we were all feeling the effects of Sammy's cancer. Day 27 needed to come soon for more reasons than one. We needed answers. More than anything we needed to know that Sammy would be okay—otherwise, we wouldn't be.

CHAPTER 28

AFTER STORMING OUT OF THE ROOM I'D PLANNED ON GOING TO THE games room and sulking. I was angry and needed to cool off but as I walked past Oliver's room I heard him call my name. I looked inside to find the whole room crowded with people. By the window there were four women sitting on the bed and they all looked strikingly similar to Oliver's mom. They wore the same long black dresses with white polka dots and white shirts beneath. Their brown hair was braided into two tight braids across their foreheads and tucked beneath their funny hats or bandanas or whatever you want to call them.

Standing at the end of Oliver's bed was a tall man wearing a wide-brimmed hat, dark pants and a sooty white shirt. He looked like he'd walked straight off a farm or the set of an old Western movie. Beside the man, like little clones, two boys stood in the exact same outfits.

Oliver was sitting on the bed with a little girl I guessed to be about three or four in his lap. She was wearing a small, black polka dot dress like the women but her hat had come untied and was tipping off her head. She smiled a big toothy smile at me as I entered.

"Meet the Walter crew," Oliver said, pointing around the room. "You know my ma, and these are my aunties," he pointed at the bed and the women nodded slightly. "And my pa, and two of my brothers, Paul and Isaiah."

The man at the end of the bed tipped his hat to me and the two little boys did the same. I wished I had a hat to tip back. That would've been fun.

"And this is the littlest Walter—Sarah. She's only three years old."

"Four!" the little girl said, looking back at Oliver indignantly.

Oliver smiled and poked her in the side. "I know, I know, I was just kidding."

The little girl giggled and squirmed in his lap as he tickled her.

I was still feeling pretty lousy about the fight between Mom and Dad and wished I hadn't walked in to Oliver's room. I just wasn't in the mood for introductions. Still, I couldn't just leave and it would have been rude not to say anything.

"You sure have a lot of brothers and sisters."

"Oh, this is only half of us," Oliver replied, as he let Sarah slide off his lap and onto the floor. She ran around the bed and jumped into her mother's lap. "I have three older brothers and an older sister back home. These are just the unfortunate three selected to come visit this week."

"Oliver!" his mother said.

It was the first time I'd heard his mother say anything.

"Sorry, Ma," Oliver said sheepishly, "I was only kidding."

I noticed Oliver's dad shifting uncomfortably back and forth in his cowboy boots. "We should probably be heading out," he said. He turned toward me and tipped his hat again. "It was nice to meet you, Cal." His two clones also tipped their hats and the three of them walked past me into the hall.

The aunts looked at Oliver's mom and she nodded. They stood, one of them grabbing Sarah's hand while she clung tightly to her mother's leg. "Go on, Sarah," I heard her mother whisper as she leaned forward and gave her a kiss on the top of her head. Reluctantly, Sarah let go and started to follow her aunts out of the room but when she was nearly out the door she broke free and rushed back in. She jumped up on the side of Oliver's bed and he helped her up. I guess even with arms like toothpicks he still had some strength. He hugged his little sister briefly before putting her back down. This time she ran back out of the room and I heard her tiny footsteps disappear down the hall.

I looked back at Oliver but there was a funny haze in his eyes. He turned and stared out the window, as if trying to hide his face.

"Were you heading to the games room?" he asked, still not looking at me.

I nodded, before realizing he couldn't see me. "Yeah," I said.

"Okay, I'll join you."

As he turned to climb out of bed I saw him quickly wipe his eyes on his sleeve. His mom came around and helped him with his IV. She walked behind us pushing the pole but left when we sat down in front of the TV and started playing Mario.

My mind wasn't really into the game so I was especially bad. I just couldn't bring myself to care. I kept thinking about Mom and Dad arguing and Sammy's growing depression.

After I'd died for the umpteenth time at the first stupid mushroom man walking back and forth between two pipes, Oliver turned to me.

"Okay, so I know you usually suck at this game," he said, "but today you're especially sucky. What's up?"

"It's nothing," I said, trying my best to focus enough to get Luigi past the mushroom man but dying again.

"It's not nothing. As a person constantly bothered, I have pretty good insight into other people's level of botheredness." Oliver lifted the area above his eyes where his eyebrows should have been, prodding me to talk.

"It's my Mom and Dad. I can't stand being around them. They're constantly fighting and I hate it."

Oliver's face changed. His normally permanent grin went serious for once.

"Already, huh?"

"Already?"

"I call it the cancer crumble. It happens to most families in here. Something about the stress of having a child with cancer breaks families down. Even my family has gone through it and we're Mennonite, our colony is supposed to be built around family."

Mennonite. That was it. I remembered where I'd seen Oliver's mom, or at least people dressed like her. We'd gone on a class field trip to a Mennonite farm back in grade three or four outside of London. The only thing I vaguely remembered was the way they dressed and the fact that they didn't use electricity—no TV, no lights, no nothing.

"Remember when I told you I've been in here longer than anyone else?"

I nodded. "Six hundred days or something."

"671 now. But that's not entirely true. There's one other person who's been here just as long as I have, not counting the doctors and nurses."

"Who?"

"My mom. She hasn't left for a single day. So how do you think that affects our family? My brothers and sisters haven't seen their mom but for weekends in over two years. It's not surprising that our family has troubles."

We kept playing Mario but now I really couldn't focus. Oliver had to remind me when it was my turn. I kept thinking about what he'd said—the cancer crumble. I hated the sound of it but I knew deep down that it was true. My family was crumbling. A wave of sadness flooded me and I guess it must have shown on my face because Oliver looked at me and for a second he looked just as gloomy. But then his face cracked and his familiar grin returned. More than that, it spread into a giant belly laugh and I looked at him. What was he laughing about? What was so funny about my family falling apart?

"A lot of comfort that was," he cackled. "Here you are telling me that you're worried about your family and I go blabbing about how awful it's been for mine. Remind me never to become a social worker." He continued laughing so hard he had to wipe his eyes because tears had formed underneath. Finally, he stopped and took on a somewhat more serious face. "Look, I wish I could tell you how to work things out—how to make everything better between your parents—but I can't. Your parents are going to have to work things out for themselves and I hope for your sake they do. I won't sugarcoat the facts: fifty percent of marriages end after a child is diagnosed with cancer. Sounds like crappy odds but in the cancer game, those aren't too bad. And you can always choose to look at it like this—fifty percent of parents stick it out together."

I hoped my parents would be in that fifty percent. If Sammy died and my parents divorced, that would be the end of everything.

"Can I ask you something else?"

"Sure. Since I'm obviously such an uplifting source of information," he said.

I laughed. "Yeah, speaking of uplifting, were you ever, umm, how do I say this, depressed from your cancer?"

"Was I ever? Man, I'm still depressed. Dying is depressing—dying for as long as I've been dying is really depressing."

"Yeah, that's what I thought," I said.

"Why? You're worried Sammy is depressed?"

I nodded.

"Why do you think that?"

"I dunno. He's just been...distant recently. Like nothing I do or say is right. I wasn't sure if it was just the medicines or the cancer or if I'm doing something wrong. I mean—I try. I really do. I ask him all the time how he's feeling and if he wants me to read him some of *The Secret Garden*—"

"*The Secret Garden*?" Oliver said, raising his arms as he interrupted. "That book is brutal."

"Well, we used to read *Goosebumps* books but he'd always get nightmares."

"So?"

"So I didn't want him getting nightmares so I chose something else. I probably could have found something a little more interesting—maybe I'll do that."

"No, no, no. Don't find something else, go back to the *Goosebumps* books—for starters—and stop asking him how he's feeling."

"Huh?"

Oliver lifted the top of his hospital gown back up as it had fallen down when he'd lifted his arms. "I may not be able to help you with your parents, but here's something I can help with. Okay, what do you think the worst part of having cancer is?"

I hesitated. I didn't want to say the word but since Oliver seemed to use it so easily I figured I could too. "Dying?"

"Hah, so the whole world thinks. Nope, not at all. We're all dying—you're dying, Dr. Parker's dying, my mom's dying—some of us are just a little faster than others. Dying isn't the worst part of cancer. Even worrying about dying isn't the worst part of cancer. The worst part of cancer changes on a weekly—sometimes even daily—basis. Let's see, this week the worst part of cancer for me was that I couldn't breathe without feeling like I was inhaling fire. Last week it was my stomach pain. The week before that my leg went numb and tingly for two days straight. And then there's always the throwing up."

I didn't understand and it must have shown so Oliver continued. "When you ask Sammy how he's feeling what does he have to do?"

I shrugged.

"Two options: either he tells you about what's bothering him, which then leads to a lengthy discussion in which he has to actively concentrate on his symptoms, or he does what most of us do, he just says he feels fine. It's quick, it's easy, it's a lie, but who cares, it saves us from a conversation we'd have to have a thousand times a day if we didn't. Watch what Dr. Parker does every time he comes in. Sometimes it's magic, sometimes it's a discussion about birthday parties, sometimes it's a joke—but he never starts off asking how we feel."

I was starting to understand. Distraction—that's what it was about. By asking Sammy how he felt I was drawing attention to the things that were bothering him. I needed to do the opposite.

"The best thing you can do is pretend Sammy doesn't have cancer at all. Stop trying to protect him from dying and just be... normal. When you get diagnosed with cancer it's like the whole world starts pitying you and treating you differently. Before I was diagnosed I'd never even seen a TV. Now look at me, I've beaten Mario so many times I could probably do it with my eyes closed. Make sense?"

I nodded. It did make sense. I felt a little better and I finally managed to get Luigi past the first mushroom man. Of course I died on the next one, but hey, small steps right? I wanted to get back to the room to talk to Sammy but before I left I had one more question for Oliver.

"Oliver," I said. "You've been here long enough to have seen a lot of kids with cancer, right?"

"671 days, dude, keep up."

"Right, then you must have some idea of which kids are going to...you know...make it and which kids are going to..."

"Die?"

"Yeah."

He didn't speak for a while. I wasn't sure if he was thinking or ignoring my question. It turned out he was thinking. "I guess I have a pretty good idea right away. I mean it's as you said, when you've seen enough of anything you begin to recognize patterns."

"So then, do you think Sammy will be okay?"

Oliver put his controller down and got up. He walked as far as his IV cord would let him and turned off the TV. He turned back toward me and I felt his icy-blue eyes penetrating me. I swallowed hard. I felt like I knew what he was going to say but then he smiled.

"Don't let him give up hope," he said, then winked at me.

I couldn't help but smile back. Oliver thought that Sammy was going to be okay. In my mind, that was just as good as any test the doctors could run.

When I went back to the room Sammy was awake, though his eyes had the familiar glaze from his medicines. They'd started treating his stomach pain with morphine so sometimes he looked a little dopey. He didn't so much smile as open the side of his mouth ever so slightly when I entered.

"I don't imagine you feel up to going to the games room?" I asked.

His face contorted momentarily then returned to its half-awake state. "No, thanks," he muttered.

"Well, how about I read some?"

He paused before shaking his head.

"Really?" I said, walking over to my cot and grabbing a book from underneath. "I was thinking we could start *Cuckoo Clock of Doom*."

His mind was drugged. It took him a few seconds to register.

"Oh, I thought you meant *The Secret Garden*."

"Nah, that book is horrendously boring."

Sammy smiled. "Yeah."

"Promise you won't have nightmares?"

"Promise."

"Shove over," I said, giving him a playful punch in the arm. He whined but shifted over the best he could amid the wires and tubes. I sat down next to him, opened the book and read the first sentence through in my head.

Okay, I thought, here goes.

Sammy was fast asleep in a few minutes but I kept reading for over an hour.

Later that night, as I lay quietly awake in my cot, I heard Sammy shift in his bed and his breathing turn irregular.

He was awake.

I sat listening for a few more minutes to be sure but it wasn't necessary, I had spent six years sleeping in the same room as my brother, I knew when he was awake.

I rolled over in my cot and got up as quietly as I could.

I walked over beside his bed and looked down at him. The room was dark but I could see two silver reflections looking up at me.

"Hi, Sammy," I said.

"Hi, Cal."

"You can't sleep?"

I saw the dark silhouette of his head nod.

"You having nightmares?"

He didn't answer. He probably thought I would be angry if he said yes. For years I'd been telling him I would only read to him if he promised not to get nightmares.

"It's okay to be scared," I said, sitting down on the side of his bed.

Still no answer.

"How about tomorrow I bring Elligator? I think I saw him under the dresser in our room. He must have got lost. I bet he'd make you feel better."

I could make out his shadowy face thinking hard. In the end it was too much to resist—he nodded.

"Okay. I'll grab him tomorrow. How about if tonight we lie together? I'm feeling kind of scared myself."

Sammy moved over in his bed and let me crawl in next to him. It was squishy but comfortable. I felt his warm, bony body pressing up against mine start to relax and his breathing turned quickly from irregular to rhythmic as he fell asleep.

Not long after, so did I.

Chapter 29

After my talk with Oliver, things were better—not great—but better. Sammy was still getting noticeably sicker by the day but at least when he was awake he wanted me around. He'd ask me to read to him, he wanted to play cards (even though I stopped letting him win) and at night, we slept side-by-side with Elligator crammed between us.

When the weekend finished and it was time to go back to school I wanted to carry things forward. I wanted to fix things with Aleta like I had fixed things with Sammy. I'd spent the previous weeks ignoring her so I knew it wouldn't be easy, but we'd grown close enough over the summer that I knew it was still possible.

Steam rose from my lips as I waited for the bus—winter was coming. I looked at my watch and started counting the number of times I breathed in a minute. Twenty-three. I'd have to ask one of the nurses if that was normal.

The bus arrived with a screech and a pop and the door opened to reveal the bus driver staring down at me. I climbed on and gave her a shallow smile and she smiled cautiously back. I took an empty seat about halfway to the back and scooted over to the window. I was really looking forward to seeing Aleta so when we pulled onto Thornton Road and she still wasn't in her usual spot at the end of the driveway I felt myself deflate like a balloon.

On Tuesday she wasn't there again and I began to worry. I thought about her walking listlessly around at recess, her vacant stare during class, and my absence. I remembered the first time we'd met, the scars on her arms, and the worrying worsened.

I spent recess in my chain-linked chair thinking. By the time the bell rang I had decided on a plan.

Dad was already waiting in his usual spot after school, car fumes sputtering out the exhaust pipe while he left the car running. He was reading a newspaper over the steering wheel as I opened the door and hopped in.

"You ready?" he asked.

"Yeah, but I need to make a stop on the way."

"Where's that?" he asked.

"I need to bring Aleta her homework from today," I lied. "She wasn't at school. Can we stop by her house?"

"Sure, it's not much out of the way."

As we pulled into the Alvarado's driveway I had an overwhelming sense of nostalgia. It felt like only the day before that I had walked that same driveway for the first time. Only back then I'd had my little lamb beside me, ready to sacrifice had anything gone wrong. I remembered Chloe's slobbering attack and the fear of meeting Mr. Alvarado for the first time. Man, things had changed so much since then.

I had to knock twice before anyone answered. Soft footsteps, the clinking of dog tags on dog collar, the gentle swing of the door, then Raquel greeted me with a surprised look on her face.

"Cal," she said, with an uneasy tone, "good to see you. I...I've heard about everything that's been going on." She looked like she might actually start to cry on my behalf. "I'm so sorry. I hope you're doing all right." She pulled me in and suddenly I found myself wrapped in the arms of someone I'd only met twice.

"I'm guessing you're here to see Aleta?" she asked, letting me go.

"Yeah," I said, brushing the hair from my eyes.

She stepped aside, letting me pass. "She's in her room."

And there I was again in the world of déjà vu. I walked up the same creaky steps, opened the same creaky door and saw the same sad wisp of a girl I'd seen in a dream long ago. Or at least that's how it felt, like reliving a dream.

Aleta must have heard me coming because she sat cross-legged on her bed and was watching the door as it swung open. She was wearing a pair of faded jeans and a plain white tank top hidden beneath a sweatshirt that was more or less falling off her shoulders. Her dark brown hair was tied over one shoulder and she was staring at me with her green, green eyes, only they were red and puffy so I knew she'd been crying. In front of her lay the notebook she carried everywhere.

"Hey," I said.

"Hey," she said back.

"I wanted to come by and make sure you were okay since you haven't been at school." I waited for Aleta to say something but she just sat watching me. "So yeah, I also wanted to apologize. Ever since everything started happening with Sammy I just felt like I needed to be alone. But...I dunno...you know how you said some things are easier not to talk about? I feel like the more I keep everything inside, the more it just seems to hurt. I guess I just wanted to come here and tell you I'm sorry for what I said. I liked it better when we were talking." I walked in and sat on the end of her bed. "I don't think I'm really making sense, am I?"

Aleta smiled. "You are."

"Good."

For a while we sat there quietly thinking. I was thinking about Sammy, I think she was thinking about something else, but then she interrupted my thoughts.

"You know when I said some things are easier not to talk about?"

I looked at her and nodded.

"I was wrong. It is better to talk about it. And that's what I've been doing—all summer."

"You have?" I said. "You mean when you went to London on Fridays? When you talked to your mom?"

Aleta shook her head. "No, when I was with you at the Secret Spot."

"Huh?" All I could remember was specifically not talking about the things that made her sad.

"With this," Aleta said, holding up the notebook. "I was using this as a way to talk about my problems." She put the notebook back in her lap and stared at it. She was biting her bottom lip like she always did when she was nervous. "I actually wanted to show you this a long time ago but I was...I guess I was self-conscious of it." She held the notebook out toward me. "Here," she said, "I want you to read it."

"You sure?" I asked, hesitating.

"Yeah."

I grabbed the book, feeling the cover beneath my fingers. It was soft and worn, obviously having had a lot of use.

"Just don't be too judgmental, I'm not a great writer."

I opened the notebook to the first page. There was a neatly written title in the centre with a short passage below.

Sarita Juana Alvarado.

This is a book about my mother. It contains all of the memories I have of the most wonderful woman this world has ever known. Though she is gone in person, these memories now written will stay with me forever.

By: Aleta Alvarado.

I looked up at Aleta. "But your mother," I said, thinking this through in my head. "You said she was still in London."

"She is—she's at the Mount Pleasant Cemetery. We go every Friday to visit her."

As I read on, I found that the journal was full of memories of Aleta's mother—a brief synopsis of a trip to the Toronto Zoo, a thorough description of her favourite outfit, even details on the sound of her voice. It felt like I was meeting a person that had died months before.

I learned that Aleta's family hadn't always been the way I knew it.

There were stories about Aleta and her sister and parents from when they'd lived in Mexico. Of trips to the beach and sunrises over the ocean. Of Aleta and Raquel yelling at tourists learning to surf in an attempt to make them fall. Of laughing and smiling and living. Everyone and everything seemed different. Even the stories about her dad made him sound almost...nice. A far cry from the stern-looking man who gave me the shivers when I looked at him in church.

There was too much to read so I began skimming pages. Apparently Aleta had moved to Canada when she was seven but had gone back to Mexico every year to visit. At least until her mother had died. Her father had refused to go back since. He had said it reminded him too much of Aleta's mother. Her sister had agreed. And this had infuriated Aleta. So she had withdrawn from school and running and friends. She had distanced herself from her father and spoken as little as possible to her sister. She described it as feeling "sunk"—like she had been thrown into the ocean with her hands and legs tied. Eventually her father and sister had come up with the plan to move to Huxbury, hoping that a change of scenery would lead to a change in heart.

Parts of the journal were written as if she were talking to her mother and near the end I came across my name. I looked up at Aleta, expecting her to grab the book back. I knew as well as anyone that you shouldn't read a girl's diary, but she didn't reach for it, she just sat there watching me, chewing her bottom lip.

I read on:

At first I was so mad that Dad and Raquel had made us move. I thought I would hate Huxbury. But to be honest, it's not too bad. The fields and openness and Lake Huron remind me of Mexico and getting away has helped somewhat in moving on with my life. I get out more, that's for sure. And guess what? I met a boy. His name is Cal and you would really like him. He's sweet like you and there are parts of him that remind me of Raquel—the old Raquel. The Raquel before she started acting like a mother and stopped acting like a sister. He has a younger brother, Sammy, separated in age by the same difference between Raquel and me, and though he sometimes pretends to be annoyed by Sammy, it's easy enough to see how much he loves his little brother. He's always looking out for him, even when he's acting like he's not. It reminds me that Raquel and Dad love me, no matter how much they frustrate me. Oh, and we found a secret spot! We go there often to swim and read and write. I hope that you can see it from wherever you are. I hope that you're still watching.

Miss you more than yesterday,

Aleta Alvarado

I stopped reading. There were a few more pages but they had become a blur. For the first time since Sammy had been diagnosed with cancer I was crying. A drop landed on the open book right next to the word Sammy so I shut it.

I wanted to say something to Aleta—something about how sorry I was that her mom had died and that she felt like her sister didn't understand and that her dad had changed, but I couldn't—all I could think about was Sammy. I opened my mouth to speak but instead a loud gasp came out. I had to fight to pull in more air and my chest felt heavy.

Aleta crawled across the bed and hugged me, her head lightly resting on my shoulder so that I could smell the vanilla scent of her shampoo.

As we sat, I realized she was crying too. My shoulder grew wet from her tears while mine continued to drop to my lap. For the first time I was no longer feeling sad for Aleta, I was feeling sad with her.

I think I could have stayed like that forever—right there on that bed with Aleta on my shoulder and Sammy safely frozen in time—not getting better but not getting sicker either. But then I remembered that time hadn't stopped and Dad was still outside waiting.

"Dad!" I said. "Shoot!" I climbed from the bed and turned to Aleta. "Come with us, Aleta. Come to the hospital with us. Please?"

She lifted her head, her thick brown hair a mess in front of her face so that her bright green eyes were half hidden.

"I, I don't think I could, Cal," she said.

"Please, Aleta?"

It looked as if I'd stuck a knife in her stomach and turned it. Guilt washed over her face but she sat unmoved on the bed.

Finally, I turned to leave. "Okay, I guess I'll see you tomorrow at school." I waited briefly for a reply but when it didn't come I left the room.

I walked down the stairs to find Dad standing in the kitchen talking to Mr. Alvarado. They both turned and looked at me but neither looked upset. Raquel was sitting at the kitchen table with a textbook and a notepad open in front of her. She smiled nervously at me.

"Sorry, Dad," I said. "I'm ready to go."

He nodded and said goodbye to Mr. Alvarado before turning to the front door. Just as we were about to leave there was a cascade of footsteps down the stairs and Aleta appeared behind us. She had changed her sweatshirt for a nicer looking sweater and was panting from her dash down the stairs.

"Dad," she said. "Can I go with Cal to the hospital?"

Mr. Alvarado opened his mouth to reply but instead looked at Dad.

"Please?" I said, holding my hands together and giving Dad the most innocent look I could.

"It's fine with me," he said.

And like that, Aleta was coming to the hospital.

CHAPTER 30

WHEN WE FIRST WALKED INTO THE HOSPITAL ROOM, I KEPT STARING at Aleta, trying to judge her reaction. I knew she must have been shocked. How could she not have been? In two and a half weeks Sammy had transformed from a healthy-looking, albeit skinnier kid, to a mostly-bald, tube-attached-to-his-face, exhausted-looking ghost of a child. But Aleta's emotions were always hard to read. She had spent months practicing the art of hiding emotion and it served her well.

Sammy was asleep so I walked over and sat on his bed, intentionally flopping down a little harder than usual to wake him. He opened his eyes and for a second didn't seem to recognize Aleta. Then he smiled, his lips dried and cracked.

"Hi, Aleta," he said.

"Hi, Sammy," she replied. "I see you have a ton of new toys."

It was true. Sammy's room was slowly becoming Oliver's. It seemed like every day of the week there was some group or team or fundraiser that dropped off a bunch of stuff for everyone on the floor. Bingo nights were only one of the many giveaways.

Aleta picked up the baseball Sammy had gotten from Dr. Parker and read the inscription.

"This ball is pretty neat," she said, looking it over.

"Cal has one too," Sammy said, his eyes suddenly bright. "They're from the London Hurr...what are they called?" Sammy asked, looking at me.

"Hurricanes," I said, stepping up beside Aleta.

"Yeah, Hurricames," he repeated.

While Aleta and Sammy continued to talk about the various toys around the room I couldn't help but feel a little jealous. The whole distraction thing seemed to come so naturally to her. She never once asked how he felt or what any of the various tubes around the room were or commented that he looked like a zombie even though he really did look like a zombie.

Dad had gone to sit next to Mom but she had quickly stood up and said she needed a coffee. It might have just been Oliver's conversation but I was acutely aware of Mom and Dad's interactions—watching for further signs of the cancer crumble.

On her way out Mom smiled and said hello to Aleta. There was still a level of awkwardness between them but at least now I understood.

Finally, Aleta and Sammy seemed to be running out of things to talk about and I could tell he was beginning to have trouble keeping his eyes open because they kept fluttering closed.

"So how are you liking Huxbury?" Dad asked.

"It's okay," Aleta said, moving around the bed.

Dad and Aleta talked for a few minutes and I waited to make sure Sammy was asleep before grabbing her by the sleeve and pulling her toward the door. "We're just going to go to the games room," I said to Dad and he nodded and grabbed his magazine. But just as we were leaving the room Sammy's eyes snapped back open with a scared look on his face.

"Where are you guys going?" he asked.

"I was just going to show Aleta the games room," I said, retracing my steps back into the room, feeling suddenly guilty.

"Oh."

Sammy looked sad.

"We won't go if you're awake," I said. "We can stay and read to you if you want?"

Sammy shook his head looking down at the bed. "No," he said, "it's fine. You guys like it better when I'm not around anyway."

I saw Aleta's expression and knew it was exactly how I looked. It was the look of someone who'd just been stabbed in the stomach.

"Why would you think that?" I said, faking confusion.

We had avoided Sammy for the whole summer. He wasn't stupid. With Aleta back, he was worried it would happen again. If I was going to have Aleta to the hospital, I was going to have to offer Sammy some reassurance.

I sat down on the bed next to him. "I'm sorry I wasn't around much this summer. It wasn't that I didn't want to hang out with you, it was just that, well, I was being selfish."

Aleta stood next to me. "I'm sorry too, Sammy," she said.

I looked at her and with a nod we made a tacit agreement. "We have somewhere we want to show you when you're better," I said.

Aleta smiled and nodded. "Yeah."

"Really? Where?" Sammy asked.

"It's a secret spot. Across the fields, behind our house. It's a long walk but it's worth it. There's a pond for swimming, a mud river for sliding and best of all, a view all the way to Lake Huron. You'll love it."

Sammy became more awake than I'd seen him in days.

"Can you tell me more?" he asked.

"Sure."

We sat at the end of his bed describing at length the shady reading trees and the taste of the sun when it was starting to set. While I dramatically re-enacted swimming and sliding, Aleta added in the occasional detail—a colour, a smell, a sound. Together we recreated our summer. Only this time, we shared it with Sammy.

When he was just about asleep—mind rotating between our world and his—I offered him a plan. I grabbed the walkie-talkies from the bedside table and put one beside him. "When you wake up, if I'm not here, call me on this. I want to know whenever you're awake so I can come back and be with you. Okay?"

"Okay," Sammy said with a smile.

We waited a few more minutes to be sure he was asleep before we left.

Chapter 31

Really, I hadn't wanted to show Aleta the games room; I had wanted her to meet Oliver. I was happy to see he was sitting in his familiar spot by the TV when we entered. Only on that day, he wasn't playing Mario, he was writing on a piece of yellow paper that he quickly crumpled up and put in his pocket when he saw us.

"Cal," he said, "and this must be your sister."

Aleta's forehead crinkled and she looked at me with a look somewhere between surprised and comical.

"I'm kidding. I just like to make it awkward when I meet someone so they don't focus on my bald head."

I laughed when I saw how confused Aleta looked. "Aleta, meet Oliver. Sometimes I think all the medications he takes affect his brain."

"They probably do," Oliver said, reaching out his hand and shaking Aleta's. "You guys are just in time. I was planning a field trip today."

"A field trip?" Aleta asked.

"Follow me," Oliver said, standing up.

I had no idea what Oliver was planning but I helped him get untangled so that he could make his way to the door. When he got to the exit he turned and put up his hand to stop us. He looked around the corner then said, "Psst, Jenny, come here."

Moments later one of the nurses appeared. She looked suspiciously at Oliver.

"Yes, Oliver?" she asked.

"You wouldn't mind letting me and a few friends out for a quick trip would you?"

The nurse looked really skeptical as she glanced over Oliver's shoulder at Aleta and me.

"Hi, Cal," she said. Then turning back to Oliver, she said, "I'm not so sure it's a good idea today."

"Ohhhh," Oliver said, grabbing his side and hunching over. "The pain is too much. I don't even know if I'll make it to tomorrow. Ohhhhhh."

Jenny rolled her eyes, turned around and looked back down the hall she had come. "Okay, just be quick," she said.

Jenny swiped her name badge over a sensor on a door and we walked through to find ourselves in a concrete stairwell. The sound inside the stairwell echoed and the only light was from a few windows on each of the floors above.

"One of you is going to have to help me with my IV pole," Oliver said, lifting the bottom of his hospital gown so that his bare legs showed beneath and started walking up the stairs. I followed behind, carefully bringing his IV pole so that I was never too far behind as to stretch the tubing and never too close as to bang his legs.

After the first flight of stairs Oliver stopped and rested against the railing.

"Phew, and I thought dying was hard work," he said, breathing heavily between words.

"Where are we going?" I asked.

Oliver turned and started up the next flight. "To the top, my friend—to the top."

It took us a while getting to the top as we had to stop longer and longer with each flight and I could sense Aleta feeling more and more worried as we went. Oliver looked ready to pass out on more than one occasion and I was beginning to realize that after this expedition, Aleta would likely never return to the hospital with me. I thought about turning around but Oliver was too determined.

At the top was a large door and Oliver grabbed a thin piece of metal off the nearby windowsill and jammed it into the frame. He was able to pry the door enough to get his fingers in, then, pushing it the rest of the way open, he said, "Welcome to my favourite spot in the whole world." Then he started to laugh. "That's a lie—but it is the nicest spot in this hospital."

A wave of cool air rushed in at us and the brightness from outside made me squint after spending the last twenty minutes walking up the dimly lit stairwell. The rooftop was flat and covered with pebbles and tar. We followed Oliver as he walked toward the far edge of the roof where he sat down with his legs dangling over the ledge.

"Grab a seat," he said, patting beside him.

I was about to say that we were fine standing when Aleta hopped up on the ledge and sat next to him. I warily joined so that the three of us were now high above the hospital overlooking the ground below. There was a parking lot directly beneath us and on the other side was a road that looped around the hospital. Opposite the road was a large, grassy park. The grass was dead and dull but the colour of the trees made up for it. A winding dirt path cut through the park, passing an old-looking playground before entering a wooded area beyond. From where we sat we could see the tops of those trees spread out like a giant quilt of oranges and yellows and greens and golds.

"Not a bad spot, huh?" Oliver said.

It wasn't quite the view from our Secret Spot, there were no rolling hills or sparkling lake in the distance, but I had to admit, it was pretty.

"It's lovely," Aleta said.

The sun was already starting its descent toward the horizon behind us and it cast a long shadow of three small figures atop the hospital on the parking lot below.

"I used to come up here a lot," Oliver mused. "Back when I used to dream of getting out. I thought that on a really clear day I might see all the way home." He pointed off in the distance to a forest on the horizon. "My colony is somewhere behind those trees."

"What do you mean when you 'used to' dream?" I asked. "What about your miracle?"

Oliver laughed. "Between you and me, I stopped waiting for a miracle a long time ago."

We sat in silence watching a man and a little girl walking hand-in-hand in the park while a white dog trotted beside them. They were heading to the playground.

Far in the distance where the horizon met the blue sky it created a sense of infinity—everything carrying on and on and on. The world was beautiful—no doubt—and I thought about bringing Sammy up to see it.

"Do you think there really is a heaven?" I asked, looking up at the sky.

Oliver shrugged and shifted a little on the edge of the roof. "Between you and me, I hope not."

Aleta and I laughed awkwardly.

I thought he must have been joking. Of course he was joking. But when I turned to face him there wasn't the slightest hint of a smile. He was just staring into the distance with a far-off look in his eyes.

"You can't be serious?" I said, repeating my thoughts out loud.

He turned and looked at me. "Why not?"

I glanced past Oliver at Aleta. This wasn't a conversation I wanted to be having in front of her. Not after what I'd just learned earlier.

"Because, if there's no heaven then where do we go after we die?"

"We get eaten by worms."

I rolled my eyes—he was definitely joking.

"No, I'm serious. What's so bad about that? What's so bad about getting eaten by worms then being recycled into the rest of the earth? Maybe my body will become part of those maple trees down there and another part will become those clouds and another part will lay hidden underground until spring when I pop out as a flower that everyone stops to look at. Or maybe I'd just be a dandelion, or a drop of water in the ocean, or a spot of dirt on someone's shoe, but you know what, I'm fine with that. I've been actively dying for a long time and the closer I get, the more I realize that this place isn't so bad—I'm fine staying."

"So then you don't believe in God?" Aleta asked.

Oliver's eyes had the same glassy look he'd had when I'd seen him with his sister. "Which god? I've been away from the colony long enough to know that there are supposedly lots of gods out there. Everyone in this hospital believes something different so why can't I? If I believed my colony's religion, then I'd be saying billions of other people were wrong. And if I believed someone else's, the same thing goes. So I've come up with my own idea for an after-life and that's just worms."

I was shocked. I'd never heard anyone say they didn't believe in God. I'd just assumed the reverend and Mom and Dad and everyone else at church knew what they were talking about.

"So what about your family? Wouldn't you miss them if you just became...dirt?" Aleta asked.

"No. They'll be right there with me when they die. Maybe they'll be a cloud next to my cloud and we'll float over Africa and see the Sahara, or we'll be swaying pines in a forest along a coast somewhere, or maybe one atom of me will get joined to one atom from each of them and we'll become a drop of water in a river that rushes down a mountain only to get evaporated at the bottom and to do it all over again."

The idea made me think about our Secret Spot and when I looked at Aleta I thought she must have been thinking the same thing because she wasn't scowling or questioning Oliver's crazy idea but actually nodding with a thoughtful look on her face.

"Yeah, that sounds nice," she said.

"I'm just not convinced that there's some unfathomably wonderful place up there that's so much better than here," Oliver continued. "I like it here. I like everything about here. I just don't like everything about my health here. But if I were just atoms there would be no more cancer, no more pain, no more dying, just me travelling the world, changing from one form to another, seeing everything I never got to see because I haven't left this hospital in 675 days."

We sat in silence watching our shadows slowly creep across the road, listening to the wind and thinking about Oliver's version of heaven, when we were pulled from our thoughts by the staticy voice of Sammy on the walkie-talkie.

"Cal? Cal, are you there?" it crackled.

I picked up my walkie-talkie and pressed the button. "Roger that. I'm here. I'll come down right away."

"Okay," he said. Then after a few seconds, "Oh, I meant robber that."

I stood up carefully and hopped off the ledge.

"I have to head back downstairs. You coming?"

Aleta stood up and followed but Oliver didn't.

"I'm going to stay out a little longer," Oliver said. "Feel free to tell Jenny I fell off the edge."

I laughed. "We won't."

"Bye, Oliver," Aleta said. "It was nice to meet you."

"And, you," Oliver said, putting his hand to his head and pretending to tip an invisible hat.

That night when we dropped Aleta off at her house she told me she would come back. We hugged outside the car but it was awkward and short—Dad was sitting in the car watching. Still, it felt nice to have Aleta back. It felt like things were finally looking up.

CHAPTER 32

THE LAST WEEK BEFORE DAY 27 SEEMED TO CRAWL BY. IT WAS like waiting for a birthday or Christmas—the more I thought about it, the longer it took.

In truth, it wasn't so much that I wanted Day 27 to come as I needed Day 27 to come. Sure, I wanted answers. I wanted to know that Sammy's cancer was better and that soon he could come home, but more so, my parents needed to know.

The tension between Mom and Dad had continued to climb the closer Day 27 got. It got to the point that they couldn't even be in the same room. When Dad came, Mom made an excuse to leave—a fundraiser meeting, a coffee, a walk—something to get out. Then when Dad went home Mom returned and sat next to Sammy on the bed, running her fingers across his head, just like she used to when he had hair, reading another book about cancer. She must have read every book on cancer possible. Which meant that she knew just about everything there was to know about Sammy's cancer. It also meant she understood when the doctors jabbered on in the mornings about platelets and red blood cells and medicines with fancy names. She knew what Sammy needed when he was throwing up or had a tummy ache or couldn't sleep. She knew tons, which meant she could answer my questions. Well, most of them.

"Mom, how long will Sammy have to stay in the hospital?" I asked one evening while I ate my cafeteria dinner on the cot.

"That depends, honey," she said, not looking up from her book.

Sammy was asleep next to her so I thought it was an okay time to ask about his cancer.

"Depends on what?" I asked.

"Well, it depends on how the cancer responds to the chemotherapy."

I knew that already. I knew we were waiting for the answer from the bone needle, but I wanted to know how long after the bone needle.

"No, I mean, like, if Sammy's bones don't have any more cancer, how long after that? Do we get to go home right away?"

Mom put her book down on her knee and looked at me. "No, it doesn't work like that. These first twenty-seven days are called induction therapy,"—I repeated the word induction in my head—"after that Sammy will need a few more months of chemotherapy to be sure it doesn't come back."

"How many more months?"

"Two, maybe three. I'm not sure exactly."

"So, no matter what, he'll still be here at least another two or three months," I whined.

"No, he could probably come home for those two or three months. He would only have to come back once a week for the chemotherapy. It's only during the induction therapy that he has to stay in the hospital."

"Why?"

"Because the chemotherapy they use during the induction therapy is very strong. His body is so wiped out that if he went home he'd be at risk for picking up an infection."

"Like the flu?"

"Yes, like the flu."

"So that's why we can't come to the hospital if we have a cold or something?"

Mom nodded.

I heard footsteps behind me and turned to see Jenny walk into the room. She began adjusting something on Sammy's IV pump. The nurses were always coming in and out.

"And what happens if his bone needle shows that the chemotherapy didn't work?"

Mom's face looked a little stern. "Let's not worry about that."

"But would he have to stay in the hospital for six hundred days?"

"Six hundred days?" Mom said. "Why would you think that?"

"Because the chemotherapy didn't work for Oliver and he's been here for 670-something days."

"Oh," Mom said. She looked like she was thinking but I guess she couldn't think of anything to say because we just sat looking at each other.

Finally, Jenny spoke from where she was still adjusting the IV pump. "You don't have to worry about Sammy being here as long as Oliver. Oliver could have left here a long time ago if he wanted."

Jenny turned and looked at the door as if she was nervous about what she'd just said. Oliver's room was right next door, I guess she was worried he might have heard.

"Oliver isn't here because he wants to be," I said a little angrily.

"Oliver can't eat without his IV or else he throws up. He's here because he needs the medicine."

Jenny lifted one eyebrow. "Really?" she asked, still going about fixing Sammy's tubing. "Have you ever seen Oliver gag or throw up?"

I was about to respond but had to stop and think. I scanned my memories for a time I'd seen Oliver throwing up. I hadn't. I hadn't even seen him look nauseous before, and I knew what that looked like because Sammy was always nauseous.

"Then why is he still here?" I asked.

Jenny shrugged. "I don't know. Only Oliver does. Anyway, I really shouldn't be telling you all of this. I just didn't want you worrying that Sammy would be here that long. Oliver is a bit of an anomaly. Not that we mind, we love having him here."

The next day at school I told Aleta about what Jenny had told me. We tried to figure out why anyone would want to stay that long in the hospital. It didn't make sense. Especially after everything Oliver had told us about wanting to see the world. You'd think if that were true he would be itching to get out. I wanted to ask him but Jenny had made me promise not to say anything.

Aleta came to the hospital twice more before Day 27. Both times she sat next to me on the cot while I read to Sammy, then after he was asleep we went out and joined the evening activities the volunteers put on. I spent most of my time thinking about Sammy and double-checking to be sure my walkie-talkie hadn't run out of batteries, but not Aleta. She got involved. It was like something changed in her at these activities. At school she hardly spoke more than a few words to anyone but at Art Night she went and sat down next to Gracie—the little girl with ALL and Down

Syndrome—and helped her make a necklace out of noodles. I guess the other volunteers must have noticed because at Pet Night she was asked to help walk the dogs around so the kids could pet them. She smiled, she laughed—something I hadn't seen her do with other people around ever. I felt happy watching her. For a little while I could take my mind off Sammy—for a short, tiny, millisecond of a while.

Then finally it arrived. The day I had waited twenty-seven days for. The day we would have our answers.

I woke up and looked outside expecting to see dark storm clouds or maybe an ominous raven sitting on the fence around our yard but all in all it looked like a pretty normal day. The sun was still shining, the sky was still blue, there were no tornados or typhoons. In fact, Day 27 looked no different from Day 26.

At school I couldn't concentrate. All I could think about were the answers we would have in a few hours. I heard Dr. Parker's voice in my head saying that the bone needle at twenty-seven days was the best indicator of how Sammy would do. If it showed no cancer, Sammy would probably be fine.

At recess I marched across the frosted grass and sat watching the other kids playing while Aleta scribbled in her journal next to me, trying her best not to look anxious. She knew it was Day 27. She knew how nervous I was. I wanted her to come to the hospital with me but we agreed it wasn't a good idea. So I drove with Dad and pretended that his hands always shook while he gripped the steering wheel.

When we got there Sammy was lying in bed, his hip covered with a square white bandage just visible through the slit in the side of his hospital gown like it had been after his first bone needle. Mom's face told me she didn't have answers yet; not happy enough for good news, not sad enough for bad, just a cardboard look of worry.

I sat next to Sammy and quickly dug through my day to retrieve something worth sharing. "Tom failed his math test this week. I saw it under mine when Ms. Draper was handing them out."

Sammy grinned.

Dr. Parker came in sometime after dinner and I knew right away that he had an answer. He walked in and sat down on the end of Sammy's bed, looking around the room. The only noise was a tiny hum from something behind Sammy's bed. I wanted to know the answer so badly. I wanted to yell, "Tell me what you know!" but then he looked directly into my eyes and I had my answer. It was all over his face. His eyes lacked their usual twinkle. It was as if he had aged a hundred years since I saw him last.

His voice was quiet as he told us that Sammy's cancer had not responded to the chemotherapy.

CHAPTER 33

I HADN'T STAYED LONG. I COULDN'T STAND BEING IN THE ROOM. You'd think I would have been overcome with sadness, like Dad whose sobs could be heard echoing around the oncology floor or Mom who sat next to Sammy rubbing his back and saying, "It's going to be all right, it's going to be all right."

Instead I was overcome with another emotion—anger.

I was angry at the chemotherapy that had poisoned Sammy's body for a whole month, taking his hair and shrinking his body but doing him absolutely no good. I was mad at the cancer. I was mad at Dr. Parker. I was mad at...

I stood up and walked quickly from the room. I walked down the hallway, glancing briefly into Oliver's room to be sure he wasn't there, then went into the games room. Oliver was sitting in his usual chair playing Mario. I walked up and turned the screen off—right in the middle of his game.

"You told me Sammy would be fine!" I yelled. "You lied to me!"

Oliver looked startled. I was screaming really loud but I didn't care. I was furious.

"I never said Sammy would be fine," he protested.

"You said to not let him lose hope! You made me believe he would be okay! But you knew all along that this would happen!

You said you could tell straight away if a kid was going to be okay. You lied to me!"

"I said to have hope, yes, but I never said he would be fine."

"Then why did you say that? Why did you make me build his hopes up if he had no hope at all? Why?"

"Because the only thing worse than dying is living without hope."

At that moment I didn't stop to think through what he'd said. I didn't stop to think that maybe Oliver was living without hope. I was too angry to think.

"You're not who I thought you were. You go around pretending like cancer and dying are no big deal but you're nothing but a scared kid. I know your secret. You could have left here months ago but instead you stay. You stay because you're too afraid to leave. Too afraid to be outside the walls of this hospital that you think protect you."

Oliver's face changed. He suddenly looked mad. "Ha! You think I like it here? You think this is some sort of safety net for me? You don't know anything. Don't come in here and pretend like you know what it feels like to have cancer."

"You're right—I don't know. But if you weren't so selfish maybe you'd see that you're not the only one affected by your cancer. Maybe your brothers and sisters would like to spend some time with you before you're gone. Maybe they're sitting at home thinking about you right now. Maybe they have a secret spot tucked away in the trees that they really want to show you. Or maybe they'd like to go on a bike ride, or play a game of tag, or just sit and read. I may not know what it's like to have cancer, but I know what it's like to be the sibling."

I seemed to hit a sensitive spot because his demeanour changed. His defensive wall crumbled and he slumped down in his chair. For a moment I just glared at him. My breathing was heavy and fast.

"It's not that easy," he said.

"What's not so easy? You tell the nurses you want to go home and you do. Seems pretty easy to me."

"I can't leave, I, I...there's..."

"There's what? Tell me!"

His eyes narrowed and he looked straight at me. "You're right. I don't leave here because I'm scared. Every moment of every day I'm afraid that I'll go to sleep and won't wake up again. I'm scared shitless of dying. There's the truth; you happy now?"

I stepped back in disbelief. I hadn't for a moment believed myself when I'd accused him of being scared. I was just angry. "Afraid of dying?" I said. "Then why do you walk around pretending like it's no big deal? What about your 'everyone is dying' speech? I thought the worst part about cancer wasn't dying, I thought the worst part was the day-to-day symptoms."

"I say a lot of things, Cal." His voice was suddenly quiet. "The symptoms suck and are by far the worst part of cancer, but dying isn't as easy as I pretend it is. The truth is I'm scared of dying because I know when I'm gone I'll miss everything. Spring planting, fall harvests, riding horses, playing hide-and-go-seek with my brothers and sisters, my parents, the colony—it'll all be gone."

"So why stay here? If you're worried about missing the colony and your family then why not spend as much time with them as you can?"

"Because the less time I spend out there, the less there will be to miss."

The anger was quickly leaving. Instead a large hole began to open in my chest but that too was filling quickly. It was like a hole dug in the sand on a beach, out of nowhere water was rising from the bottom—the sadness was beginning to seep in. I felt suddenly exhausted and flopped down in the chair next to him.

For a while we just sat in silence until another thought came to me.

"What about your heaven? What about the idea of becoming clouds and trees and a part of everything again?"

Oliver nodded slowly. "Yeah, it's a nice thought, huh?"

I closed my eyes and put my head back on the seat.

"Yeah," I said. "It is."

I cried quietly in the chair next to Oliver. Normally I hated crying in front of anyone, but for some reason I just didn't care. I felt the tears running down my cheeks, wetting the neck of my shirt. I thought about Sammy and Oliver and all the other kids who had cancer. It wasn't fair. Then again, I guess I'd known right from the start that cancer wasn't fair, and Sammy was just never lucky with anything.

I was pulled from my miserable daydreaming by the sound of my mother's voice.

"Are you okay, Calvin?" she asked.

I looked up at her. She was standing in the doorway of the games room and looked anything but okay herself.

"I'm fine," I said.

"Do you want to come back now?"

"Is Sammy awake?" I asked.

She nodded.

"Okay."

I stood up and walked to the door but Oliver's voice stopped me.

"Cal," he said.

"Yeah?"

"I'm sorry about Sammy."

CHAPTER 34

THE ONLY THING WORSE THAN DYING IS LIVING WITHOUT HOPE.

I kept Oliver's words with me after Day 27. Sometimes it was hard—very hard—but I saw it as my job to make sure Sammy didn't give up. Probably because I wasn't ready to give up.

"There are other options and we will try them all if we have to," Dr. Parker explained.

"What other options?" Dad asked.

"There are different chemotherapies, higher doses—we'll come up with a plan but as I said, things will be more difficult now that induction therapy has failed. The cancer is spreading and Sammy is weaker—still, we won't give up hope."

"What about transplant?" Mom asked.

Dr. Parker shook his head. "In order to transplant we'd have to get rid of the cancer first. You have to wipe everything out in order to plant new seeds. We need to try to induce remission, otherwise, even transplant isn't an option."

So we tried.

But no matter how many different or stronger or longer chemotherapies they threw at it, Sammy's cancer didn't seem to get any better. His body only shrivelled further and his symptoms only worsened.

We stopped counting the days. There was no more mystical Day 27 where things would be better. Instead we stuck to our routine, hoping for a miracle. For me that consisted of school followed by the hospital, school followed by the hospital, over and over and over again.

There were a few special days that stick out in my memory but even they didn't seem so special. Mom's birthday passed without anyone noticing it. Dad was always the one who made a big deal of it, reminding us to draw cards or make gifts, but either he forgot or just didn't want to bother. There was a birthday party for a new patient put on by her parents, but Sammy couldn't eat any cake so I just felt bad. Christmas was disappointing. Mom decorated the room and Dr. Parker showed up wearing a Santa costume but Sammy wasn't feeling well enough to leave the room for the party in the games room so we stayed in our usual four-wall enclosure and exchanged gifts there.

Sammy was sitting on his bed wearing a Santa hat, the white fluff all but covering his eyes as he peered out beneath.

"Who goes first?" I asked, sitting next to him with a wrapped gift in my lap.

Sammy looked up at Mom like he'd forgotten his homework somewhere.

"Do you have it?" he asked her.

Mom handed him a small package the size of an egg. I could tell by the wrapping that Sammy had done it—there was about an entire roll of wrapping paper and two rolls of tape used to close it.

He handed me the tiny package. "You go first," he said.

His eyes watched me closely as I unwrapped it. It took a while—

I had to peel off the tape piece by piece—but when I finally got it open a keychain fell out into my lap. On it was a small coin the size of a quarter. One side of the coin was smooth silver while the other had a small painting of a bald eagle in midflight.

"Do you like it?" Sammy asked. "It has an eagle on it just like you. It was only fifty cents from the gift shop. Mom paid for it."

"It's great. I love it," I said, but I felt a tightness in my throat as I said it. I leaned over and hugged him. "Thanks, Sammy."

Next I handed him the gift from my lap. He needed Mom's help getting it open and inside was a copy of *The Headless Ghost*.

Sammy looked at the cover.

"It's a new *Goosebumps* book!" he exclaimed.

"Brand new!" I said. "It's called *The Headless Ghost* and it just came out. I haven't even read the first page or anything."

"Will you read it to me?" he asked, handing me the book.

I pushed it back toward him. "Nope."

He looked confused. "But I can't read it."

"Not yet," I said. "But when you're old enough to read I want you to read it to me. Until then, I'm not going to read it myself."

Hope, I thought, don't let him lose it.

CHAPTER 35

It was some time shortly after Christmas that Sammy's condition took a sharp turn for the worse. His lungs began to hurt when he breathed, his legs became too weak to walk so we had to push him around in a wheelchair, his eyes never looked fully open and he hardly smiled anymore. Every part of him was falling apart bit by bit.

Dr. Parker sat across from Mom and Dad in our room while Sammy slept and I watched TV. I knew Dr. Parker had come to say something important because Mom and Dad hardly ever sat together anymore and they both looked nervous. I listened to what they were saying instead of watching Ninja Turtles.

"I wanted to talk to you about a plan," Dr. Parker said. "As you know, the chemotherapies aren't working. The cancer has continued to grow and at some point we need to start thinking about other options."

"What do you mean, other options?" Dad asked.

"What I mean is, there comes a point when we need to stop fighting a losing battle. At some point we need to change our focus from trying to get rid of the cancer to keeping Sammy comfortable. As you know, the chemotherapies have side effects and if they aren't working we're only doing more harm by giving them." Dr.

Parker sighed, pushed his glasses up on his nose, and looked at my parents. "It is the consensus of the oncology team that the medications are not going to work going forward and we should consider making Sammy palliative."

Palliative.

It meant we were done trying to treat Sammy's cancer.

"But there are other things we can try," Mom said, her voice sounding suddenly frantic. "There's a trial going on in Georgia looking at a new medication that blocks a receptor or something important for the AML cells to grow. I have the article—" Mom's hands shook as she reached for a book beside the bed.

"I know the trial," Dr. Parker said. "It's being run by an old colleague of mine. It would not benefit Sammy. The medication is only useful once remission has been induced. It is used to prevent relapses. It wouldn't help Sammy." Dr. Parker was shaking his head slowly and looking at the floor. I watched out of the corner of my eye, afraid that they would stop if they knew I was listening. Dr. Parker looked back up at Mom and Dad and continued, "We have already exhausted all the possible research trials that may benefit Sammy. We have gone through two medications still in the research phase and neither has worked. At this point, there is nothing more we can offer." Dr. Parker looked like he was saddened by the sound of his own voice.

"Transplant," Mom said. "What about a transplant?"

Dr. Parker shook his head.

Mom looked at Dad, her eyes wild with fear. "Then there are alternative therapies. Down in Mexico there's someone offering a natural treatment for leukemia. It's expensive but—"

Dr. Parker raised his hand to interrupt. "If you wish to look into alternative therapies I won't stop you. But I can tell you this, with Sammy's cancer as it is, they will not offer a cure. They are expensive and poorly researched. Many are nothing more than a scam. If you wish to look into them, I'd be happy to help, but honestly, I think it is in Sammy's best interest to start focusing on comfort measures."

"We appreciate your opinion but—"

Mom stopped when Dad put his hand on hers. "Liz," he said, his voice shaking in the back of his throat, "don't you hear what he's telling us? We're just going to make things worse for Sammy. We need to focus on—"

Mom tore her hand away abruptly. "You!" she said, but the rest of the sentence didn't come out. She stood up and started to leave. She turned back at the door, her eyes full of tears. Mom hardly ever cried in front of me, sometimes I'd see her wipe her eyes when we'd first walk into the room, but she wasn't like Dad, she didn't cry often. "You already gave up months ago," she said, pointing at Dad, then stormed out of the room.

Not long after, Dr. Parker and Dad left too.

It was one of the few times I was happy Sammy wasn't awake.

The next time I saw Mom and Dad was later that evening and when I asked what they had decided I knew from the quietness of the room what the decision had been.

Palliative.

It would become my least favourite word in the English language.

So I sat by for the next few weeks as my brother turned into a tiny trace of a human boy. His skin became yellow and his breathing raspy. He sounded like he constantly had something stuck at the back of his throat and the nurses would have to pinch his fingers to wake him up. I remember him being so small—so, so, so small.

Mom became more involved; Dad became less. I started thinking of them less as my parents in the plural form and more as separate entities. They probably spoke ten words to each other over those last few months. If it wasn't for Aleta I might never have made it. Everywhere around me life was falling apart and she remained the only constant.

At school I wasn't expected to contribute. No one cared if my homework wasn't done. No one would have even cared if I didn't show up. So I just sat there and did what I always did—worried about Sammy. I worried constantly. At night I'd be afraid to close my eyes and if I did I'd wake up shortly after in a cold fit. Sometimes I'd be screaming and Dad would come in to make me feel better. Only there was nothing he could say to make me feel better.

Then it happened. I feel terrible even writing it down. It was a mistake—an honest to God mistake. I can't say why I did it. Maybe I was tired? Maybe I was too worried? I'm not sure and I don't think I'll ever know. It's just something I'll always have to live with.

When I woke up that morning with a headache I didn't think much of it. It wasn't even that bad. It was the kind of thing you notice at first but forget about pretty quickly. Same with the stuffiness in my nose; I didn't even need to blow it or anything. Just the occasional sniffle here and there.

So when I went to the hospital that day and they asked me if I was feeling okay, I just nodded and washed my hands like I always did.

My mistake didn't even occur to me until four days later when

I was sitting in school listening to Ms. Draper discuss something about geography.

It was a cold March day and a gust of snow and chilled air entered the portable as the door at the back opened. Twenty heads turned around, eager for an excuse to forget their geography textbooks, and there stood my Dad with the principal.

No words needed to be said. His expression said enough.

An overwhelming panic overtook me as we walked toward the car. I felt lightheaded. I felt my stomach clench like someone was jumping up and down on it. I felt my heart beating out of my chest and my knees turn to rubber. I fell into the backseat of the car.

We drove at a dangerous speed to the hospital and left the car in the no-parking area at the front. When we entered Sammy's room he had a new tube running from his nose to a small canister on the wall. The label above it read 'oxygen' in green lettering.

It wasn't so much that Sammy looked different as it was that he sounded different. I could hear him breathing all the way from the door. It was like his lungs were trying desperately to suck every drop of oxygen from the wall.

Dad and I stood frozen in the doorframe. It was me who moved first. I walked up to Sammy and watched. He was exactly how I imagined someone might look after nearly drowning—white, wet, struggling to breathe with lungs that sounded full of water.

I heard Dr. Parker's voice from behind me like God narrating.

"He has pneumonia—an infection of his lungs. Only his body has no way to fight it and his lungs are too weak."

In not so many words he was telling us that it was the end.

I wondered if Dr. Parker knew I had given Sammy the pneumonia. He was a doctor—of course he knew. I didn't turn around. I imagined his voice in my head, "It's your fault. It was you who came to the hospital with a cold. It was you who gave Sammy pneumonia."

And it was true.

I was the one who gave Sammy pneumonia.

I stared at Sammy.

If this was the end, I thought, why was he so calm? Why wasn't he scared or fighting or screaming like I'd imagined so many times before? Why was he always so much stronger than I was?

I couldn't bear them standing behind me anymore.

"Mom, Dad," I asked, "do you think I could have a second alone with Sammy? I want to tell him something."

I waited for their footsteps to leave and the door to close, then sat down next to Sammy.

"Sammy?" I said, but he didn't move. There was no response.

I shook his shoulder hard, begging him to wake up.

"Please, Sammy, wake up, I need to talk to you."

I grabbed his hand. It felt like bones and skin, nothing more, and it was cold. I squeezed it hard but there was no reaction.

His head moved up and down each time he breathed and there was a space right under his neck that seemed to suck all the way back each time.

I pinched his arm and he moaned a little, pulling away.

"Sammy," I said, putting my mouth right next to his ear. "Wake up. Please wake up. I want to give you a Level. Come on, open your eyes, just for a minute."

His eyelashes fluttered briefly then opened. He looked around the room but it was a vacant stare. Finally, his eyes found mine but I had a feeling like he didn't know who I was. At least his face didn't light up like it always used to and there was no knowingness in his eyes. It was a horrible, empty look.

"Sammy," I continued, "the committee has decided to award you the highest Level possible." My vision blurred and my cheeks began to burn with hot tears as I spoke. "Based on months of IVs and pain and nausea and bone needles, all without complaint, and years of being the best brother anyone could ever ask for, I...err...we, the committee, have decided to award you the Level of Dragon."

Sammy eyes focused and he stared at me intently. It was the longest he'd kept his eyes open in weeks. His voice was fragile as he spoke. "I thought Eagle was the highest Level?"

"Eagle *was* the highest Level," I replied.

I wanted to come clean. I wanted to tell Sammy that I didn't deserve the highest Level. I didn't deserve any Level. I'd never done a single brave thing in my life. While he had lived every day putting up with the abuse, first from his older brother, then from cancer, I'd lived a life of self-proclaimed greatness. It was time to own up to the fact that Sammy, five years my junior, was ten times my superior, and this was the only way I could think to tell him.

"Are you a Dragon?" he asked.

I wiped my eyes on my sleeve. "No, I'm still an Eagle," I said.

For a moment he didn't say anything and I was worried he was slipping off into the emptiness again.

Finally, he said something but it was so quiet I couldn't hear. I leaned in really close so that my ear was right next to his mouth.

"What?"

"Can I be an Eagle, too?" he whispered again.

It didn't matter to me. Sammy could be any Level he wanted to be. If all he wanted was to be an Eagle, he could be an Eagle.

"Sure," I said. "You're an Eagle."

His lips formed a smile as he rested his head back on his pillow and closed his eyes. Beneath his arm he clung tightly to his Elligator.

Later that night as I lay beside him holding his hand, I heard Sammy's breathing turn from irregular to regular and then stop forever. And my world shattered into a million horrible pieces.

CHAPTER 36

FRAGMENTS.

My memories of the funeral are only fragments. Probably because that is how they came to me.

Pieces of a church with stained glass windows and white, peeled paint. The church was full of people—more people than could fit inside. They had stood against the walls and in the aisle and outside the doors—they'd had to leave the doors open.

I remember the smell of burnt candles and pine garlands drowning out the familiar stench of farm animals as we sat waiting for Reverend Ramos to start. But I couldn't focus on the reverend behind the altar. Instead I kept staring at the small, steel-sheet coffin beside him.

I kept thinking about Sammy; kept reminding myself that he wasn't next to me, that he was in that coffin. I thought back to the time we had gone to Mr. Wilson's funeral and hoped the casket would be open. We had hoped to see a dead body. Sammy's coffin was closed and I thanked God for that.

When I couldn't stand looking at the coffin any longer I turned and started scanning the crowd. I found Aleta sitting four rows behind me, sandwiched between her sister and father. Her eyes met mine and held them. She gave me a slight nod and I nodded back. Beneath her eyes were tiny pools of water. I had seen her cry before; only this time it was different, she wasn't crying for her mother, she was crying for Sammy—and for me, I think.

I felt my own eyes begin to well so I looked away, scanning the crowd for more familiar faces. There were lots of kids from school, a few more from London, and near the back was a row of nurses and doctors from the hospital. Dr. Parker was among them. He was wearing a grey suit with a black tie. I'd never seen him wearing a suit before. He'd worn ties in the hospital, but they had always had fun things like dogs or Star Wars or cartoons on them, never just black. He looked old and tired and he was no longer smiling.

I got the sense that Reverend Ramos was about to start because people began to hush but before I turned around my eye caught someone else I recognized. They were standing along the side of the church—a tall, broad man with two smaller silhouettes in front of him. The man had a hand on each of the boys' shoulders—Joey and Tom. It might have been my imagination, I didn't have time to look for very long, but to this day I'm convinced the two meanest boys in our school had tears in their eyes.

Reverend Ramos started talking—something about God and heaven and Sammy. He said that Sammy was up above with people that loved him and that God would make a special place for him there. It made me sad to think of Sammy so far away. I liked Oliver's version of heaven better. Sammy wasn't going to God's heaven, Sammy was going to be buried in the ground and stay with me. He would be in the clouds and rain and grass—just like Oliver said. Sammy wasn't going anywhere.

When the reverend started reading something from the Bible

my mind completely left the church. I don't remember what I was thinking, only that I snapped back out of it when he said something with an 'R' in it. I leaned over, ready to repeat it to Sammy in my funny pirate voice, only to find Dad sitting where Sammy should have been. It wasn't the last time I'd forget my brother was gone.

I looked up at Dad. His face was bright red like he'd just run to the Secret Spot and two steady streams of tears were running down his cheeks. In his lap was a pile of tissues as high as his stomach and every so often he'd make a horrible noise as if he were coming up for air.

I leaned over and whispered, "It's okay, Dad, Sammy's not in heaven."

Dad looked down at me but he didn't seem to understand. He looked confused. I wanted to explain but couldn't—churches aren't for talking; they're for being quiet.

I looked over at Mom. She was sitting on the other side of me and was crying too. Only she wasn't so obvious about it. Instead she was sitting rigidly watching the reverend and moved quickly to dab her eyes with the balled up Kleenex every few seconds. She must have felt me watching her because she looked down at me with a sad look, then reached over and grabbed my hand. She squeezed it tightly. It hurt but I didn't mind. It felt nice to be held that tightly.

I was glad when Reverend Ramos stopped talking and closed the Bible. I thought we would be able to leave. I thought I could finally stop looking at that horrible coffin. Instead he looked to the back of the church.

"We have one more person who has asked to say something," he said. "Oliver, if you want to come up."

Oliver? I thought for sure it was a different Oliver than I knew but when I turned around, sure enough, there was Oliver from the hospital making his way through the crowd. He must have been near the back because I hadn't seen him.

He looked different—very different. He wasn't wearing a hospital gown but real clothes. He had on black dress pants with suspenders over a white button shirt and in his hands he carried a black, wide-brimmed hat held tightly to his chest. He was moving slowly, having to push through all the people in the aisle to get to the front.

When he got to the altar he pulled out a piece of crinkled, yellow paper from his shirt pocket and took his time flattening it out on the podium. When he was satisfied he looked up—except he didn't look up at everyone, he looked up at me.

"This is a poem," he said, "by Mary Elizabeth Frye:

Do not stand at my grave and weep
I am not there; I do not sleep.
I am the thousand winds that blow,
I am the diamond glints on snow,
I am the sunlight on ripened grain,
I am the gentle autumn rain.

When you awaken in the mornings hush,
I am the swift uplifting rush
Of quiet birds in circled flight.
I am the soft stars that shine at night.
Do not stand at my grave and cry,
I am not there; I did not die."

CHAPTER 37

On the top of a hill, in a cemetery in London, we buried Sammy beneath a leafless poplar tree. A small patch of ground was cleared of snow and in the centre a hole the size of a child's coffin was dug. To this day I'm not sure how they dug a hole in the frozen earth, but there it was, as if the ground had just opened up to swallow my brother.

Afterwards people came up to me and Mom and Dad to say how sorry they were. They kept talking about how bravely Sammy had fought. They kept referring to "Sammy's fight with cancer." To me it didn't seem like much of a fight—more like a bully beating up a little kid who sat with his arms tied behind his back. I thought about telling them this but decided not to—the less I said, the sooner people would leave.

I found Aleta standing off to the side after the service was over. We stood for a moment looking at each other, she in her pea coat, hair tied back in a black bow; me in a black suit Mom had bought me the day before. I didn't know what to say to her. I didn't know what to say to anyone. Which is why I was happy when she took two steps toward me and wrapped her arms around my neck.

I broke down. All the tears I'd held back in that stuffy church came rolling out like waterfalls. My body began to convulse like a car sputtering fumes.

We must have stood like that for a long time because when we finally stopped and looked around most of the crowd had disappeared. A few people in huddled groups stood around talking—Mr. Alvarado with my dad, Mom with a group of ladies from her fundraising group, Reverend Ramos and Dr. Parker—but for the most part, everyone was gone.

I hadn't noticed anyone behind me and was startled by a tap on my shoulder. When I turned around I found Oliver. He was wearing the wide-brimmed hat he was carrying in church and I'm not sure I would have recognized him out of context. He must have been waiting for us to stop crying.

"Hey, Cal," he said.

"Hi, Oliver."

He fidgeted with his hands as he spoke. "I just wanted to say that I'm sorry. Sammy deserved better. It's not fair."

I nodded unenthusiastically.

He stopped fidgeting and stood staring at me for a while. Finally, he let out a long sigh, then turned around to see if anyone was listening. He turned back and said, "Look, I know there's nothing I can say that will make you feel any better so I won't pretend to. Sammy is gone and that's the worst thing I can imagine. Dying is as bad as it gets. I could tell you that he's not suffering anymore, and there's something to that, take it from someone who's been suffering for years, but even that won't make you feel any better. So I just wanted to let you know that I'm thinking of him and of you. I'll be praying that your family is okay."

I nodded. I knew what he was talking about—the cancer crumble. It almost seemed inevitable but I didn't want to think about that right then.

"And here, I wanted to give you this."

He reached into his breast pocket and pulled out the yellow, crinkled paper.

"Your version of heaven?" I asked.

He nodded.

"Don't you want to keep it?"

"Nah, I've already got it up here," he said, pointing to his head.

I took the piece of paper between my fingers.

Oliver glanced over his shoulder and I followed his eyes. At the bottom of the hill was a small woman standing alone—Oliver's mom.

"Back to the hospital?" I asked.

Oliver turned back around and smiled. He waved his hand up and down, gesturing at his clothes. "No," he said, "I'm going home."

I smiled. "Good."

Aleta and Oliver hugged, then he stood in front of me awkwardly for a moment. I put out my hand to shake his but instead he pulled me in for a hug too. His shirt smelled musty and his body was still a birch tree with branches.

"Thanks," he said, "for everything."

I watched him walk down the hill to his mom and that was the last I ever saw him. I don't know how long he lived, or if he's still alive somewhere, but I hope that one day we'll meet again in a drop of rain somewhere—just like he said.

When everyone had said all there was to say, and all the tears that would come had come, Mom, Dad and I were left standing alone with Sammy. Mom hugged me tightly from behind as we stared at the little mound of dirt. I wasn't ready to leave but the silence was killing me so I pulled out the copy of *Cuckoo Clock of Doom* from my jacket pocket and looked up at Mom and Dad. They nodded and I opened it to the last chapter—Sammy's favourite.

I read.

CHAPTER 38

WHEN THE FUNERAL WAS OVER AND THE HOSPITAL VISITS became a thing of the past, all that was left was a broken family in a yellow-bricked farmhouse on the outskirts of nowhere.

Dad started a rebellion against the world and spent most days in his upstairs office. Sometimes I'd forget he was even there. Mom took a different approach—she became so overbearing it was suffocating. When Sammy was sick I had complained that I'd felt forgotten, suddenly I had the opposite problem.

"Where are you going? When will you be home? Are you meeting Aleta? Do you want me to pack you snacks? Promise me you'll be back before it gets dark?"

She wanted me to see a grief counsellor, and talk to Reverend Ramos, and join a soccer league, but all I wanted was to be left alone.

So I found ways.

After school I'd get off the bus, leave my bag by the front door and just walk. I'd never really know where I was going but that didn't matter. I'd walk through the woods, and through the frozen, empty fields, and sooner or later I'd turn up at the tree house in the woods. I didn't know where I was walking but I knew why.

I was looking for Sammy.

I kept thinking about Oliver's version of heaven and trying to find signs that my brother was still around. I looked everywhere—everywhere but the Secret Spot. I couldn't bring myself to go back there. An invisible wall of guilt kept me away.

So instead I'd lie down in the middle of a big open field and stare up at the passing clouds and think, that one, no, that one. But it never really felt like Sammy was there.

Other days I'd go inside the tree house and open the wooden chest where we kept all our *Goosebumps* books.

"Which one should we read today?" I'd say, then I'd choose the one I thought Sammy would pick.

I'd read out loud just like I used to and when I'd come to a word I thought Sammy wouldn't know I'd stop and say, "Hideous, it means really ugly or disgusting or something like that."

As the days rolled on I began to give up hope that I would ever find my brother. I started thinking Oliver was wrong. I felt cheated. I grew angry.

I'll never find him, I thought.

Until the day I did.

I had been sitting beside the river thinking about all the hours Sammy and I had spent fishing in that tiny stream with rods of sticks and string.

"I can't believe we actually thought we might catch something," I said, forcing a laugh.

I thought I heard Sammy laughing too, but when I stopped and listened carefully it was just the sound of the wind rushing between the trees.

I leaned over the river and started to cry. I watched as my tears fell into a still pool at the side of the river, obscuring the image of my face beneath. I cried for so long I forgot what I was crying about.

Then it happened.

I found him.

Sammy.

One second I was watching my tears fall, the next I was staring into the eyes of my brother. His dark brown hair falling over his forehead, his chubby cheeks dimpling with a smile.

"Sammy!" I said. "Sammy!"

He was trying to say something back to me but I couldn't hear him.

"What? Oh, I know," I said, "you want to read a *Goosebumps* book. Hold on."

I ran to the tree house and climbed up the ladder. The chest of *Goosebumps* was in the corner and I looked through it, tossing book after book aside as I tried to find the one that I thought Sammy would want. I couldn't make up my mind so I grabbed the rope handle on the side of the chest and pulled it toward the ladder. I walked around the other side and pushed it out of the tree house so that it landed with a thud at the bottom that echoed through the trees and sent birds rushing to the sky.

When I had pulled the box all the way from the tree house to the river I sat down again. I reached inside and grabbed the first *Goosebumps* book I laid my hands on and started to read. I read for ten minutes before putting the book down in my lap and leaning over to check on Sammy.

Only, he wasn't there anymore. Instead I saw only my stupid refection staring back at me.

"Sammy?!" I yelled, reaching my hand into the water. It was

freezing. My reflection vanished for a moment then returned a few seconds later when the water calmed. "Sammy?! Come back!"

I was suddenly furious.

"Sammy, where are you?!"

I looked again but he still wasn't there. My heart began to race. I felt abandoned. I was panicking.

I stood up and threw the book I'd been reading into the water, hitting my reflection hard so that the water rippled and jumped. When it calmed again it was only me staring back. I reached into the box and grabbed another book. This time I ripped it in half before throwing it into the water. Again, only my reflection returned. I kept reaching into the box, pulling out *Goosebumps* after *Goosebumps*, tearing them down the spine, shredding the pages, ripping the covers, then hurling them at my image.

The river became a morgue of floating books. I kept going until there were no *Goosebumps* left.

I looked back into the water.

Me.

Only me.

Sammy, I thought. Why did we have to look so much alike?

CHAPTER 39

I WALKED BACK TO THE HOUSE, MY BODY STILL TENSE WITH RAGE.

When I heard my parents' voices coming from the kitchen my anger grew.

They were fighting. They were always fighting. It was like the world was made of flint—everything provided a spark.

"Well, it certainly feels like I'm alone!" I heard Mom yell as I got closer.

"Liz, I don't know what you want me to say. I don't know what you want me to do," Dad said back, calmer and quieter, but with bitterness.

"I want you to give a damn, that's what I want. I want you to stop hiding in your office all day, I want you to come to church with us on Sundays, I want you to go see a therapist, I want you to start being a father to your son."

I reached the house and leaned back against the brick wall, listening to their voices through the kitchen window.

"I'm trying, aren't I? I read that book you gave me."

"Twenty pages," Mom replied, "you read twenty pages."

"A lot of help those twenty pages were. And what about you? You're off at your fundraiser meetings every night of the week and that's okay?"

"At least it gets me out of the house!"

"Maybe I don't want to leave the house!"

"No, maybe what you want is for me to leave! At least that's how it feels! If you're intentionally trying to push me away then just say so! Because at this point, I don't really think a divorce would be all that different!"

I'd had enough—the fighting, the constant hints at divorce, I'd heard this over and over and over. Every morning before I'd get out of bed, every night before I'd climb back in. It was another reason I left every chance I could. I wanted to be away from it all. I didn't want Mom to leave—I wanted to leave. I wanted to run away and never come back. But right then, more than anything, I wanted them to shut up.

I bent down and grabbed a rock wedged under the side of the house and took a few steps back. I threw the rock at the kitchen window before I'd really had time to think about what I was doing.

The glass shattered as if it had been struck by lightning and the rock ricocheted off something metal inside.

I didn't even have time to run before their faces appeared through the broken glass.

"Cal?" Mom said, her voice more surprised than angry.

"Maybe you should just leave!" I yelled. "Or better yet, how about I just leave!"

"Cal—" Dad said, but I didn't hear anything else. I turned and ran as fast as I could. I ran through the yard and into the dead, frozen fields beyond. I ran until I couldn't run anymore and then I walked. It was cold out and the sweat I'd worked up from running quickly turned to ice. By the time I arrived at Aleta's house I was shivering.

Mr. Alvarado opened the door but I was too cold to be scared. Anyway, he looked more worried than scary at that moment.

"May I please talk to Aleta," I said, through chattering teeth.

He brought me inside and told me to sit at the kitchen table while he made me hot chocolate and wrapped a blanket around me. Aleta came downstairs looking just as worried and sat next to me. After we had finished our drinks and the feeling returned to my fingers and toes, we were allowed to go upstairs to Aleta's room.

We sat on her bed and I told her everything.

"I can't stand it. They fight all the time and it drives me crazy. I shouldn't have thrown the rock but...I dunno...sometimes I just feel so angry. Angry with Dad for never being around, angry with Mom for nagging, angry with myself for...for...well, for being the reason Sammy's gone."

Aleta looked shocked. "What do you mean?"

I took in a deep breath—I hadn't told anyone. "You know how Sammy died from pneumonia? Well, I'm the one who gave it to him. I...I didn't know, I mean, I did but I didn't think about it. I had a cold and went to the hospital. He got my cold and it turned into pneumonia. I'm the reason he's gone."

Aleta shook her head. "Don't say that. It's not right. And it doesn't help, that's for sure."

"How would you know?"

"I used to say the same thing after my mom died," Aleta said.

"You did?"

She nodded.

I'd wanted to ask her a thousand times how her mother had died but it had never felt right. Suddenly I felt like she wanted to tell me.

"How did she die?" I asked.

She paused. "In a car accident," she said. "She was driving me to school. It was snowing that morning and the roads were covered. As we turned into an intersection I saw him coming. I remember thinking he was coming toward us so fast that he might not be able to stop, but I didn't say anything—at least not until it was too late. There was no time for my mom to do anything." She stopped for a moment, still staring down at the bed. Finally, she looked back up at me. "It took me a long time to remember even that much, afterwards it's only blank. I woke up in the hospital."

I wanted to say something intelligent. Something to make her feel better but all that came out was, "Oh."

She didn't seem to mind. Maybe it felt good to finally tell someone.

"Afterwards I blamed myself. Why hadn't I yelled sooner? Why had I lived and she died? I started to wish I was dead too."

"And that's why you have these?" I said, reaching forward and pulling up her sleeve to reveal the rows of thin scars on her arm.

She nodded.

"So what makes those thoughts go away? What makes it better?"

"Honestly," she said, "nothing."

I had hoped for some revelation. Some magical way to make the pain go away, but who was I kidding, Aleta was still hurting and always would be. I knew that.

"It gets easier though. It's almost sad in a way but you stop thinking about it as much and start thinking about other things. You start to remember the happy times instead of focusing on the what-ifs and whys. And you can do some things to help that."

"Like what?"

"Like writing down all the memories—when you're ready."

I didn't feel ready.

"And you can start doing things you enjoy again. Which brings me to something else I wanted to ask you."

"What's that?"

"I've put in an application at the Children's Hospital to start volunteering there. I was wondering, or hoping, that you'd want to come as well. I know it might not be easy to go back there but—"

"I don't think I could right now," I said, shaking my head.

She nodded that she understood. "Okay, just tell me when you're ready—for both things."

CHAPTER 40

Aleta and I spent the rest of the evening doing a puzzle on her floor when Mr. Alvarado poked his head in to say that Dad was waiting out front to take me home. I was dreading the conversation I knew was coming. I figured I would be in trouble for breaking the window.

But when I got in the car Dad didn't look mad at all. He looked something else—nervous maybe?

We drove a little ways without saying anything but I knew he wanted to speak because he kept glancing at me in the rear-view mirror and seemed to be driving illegally slow.

"Cal," he finally said, breaking the silence. "I, umm, about what happened." He cleared his throat. "About what you said. Umm, you're right about your mother and I—we shouldn't be fighting. It's not fair to you. I know how hard this has been on you so I'm—"

"How could you know?" I interrupted. "You never leave your office."

Dad stopped talking and I immediately regretted what I'd said. I knew how hard everything had been on him. I knew how hard Mom was on him. I shouldn't have joined her side but I just had.

For a minute Dad drove on then suddenly the car pulled over

and stopped—right on the side of the highway. I was sitting in the back seat and couldn't see Dad's face but I knew by the soft sobs that he was crying.

"I'm sorry, Cal," he said, but his voice was shaky. "I know I haven't been there for you these last few months. I'm trying my best—I really am—but I, I just feel so tired all the time." He wiped his eyes on his sleeve and turned toward me. It is the worst thing in the world to see your father cry and I realized I was crying too. "I just miss your brother so much and I...it's no excuse. I'm going to try harder. You'll see, I will."

"I don't want you and Mom to get divorced," I said. "I didn't mean what I said earlier."

He nodded. "I know. We both know. We talked after you left—we're going to try not to fight anymore."

"Maybe you should go see the counsellor like Mom thinks," I suggested.

He looked at me momentarily then nodded.

"Okay, I'll give it a try. Maybe we can all go."

"Okay," I said under my breath. I wasn't keen on going to talk to someone, but if it meant that Mom and Dad might be better, I'd go. I'd do anything to stop the cancer crumble.

We pulled into the driveway and the car stopped. Before I got out I said, "Dad?"

"Uh huh?"

"I know you miss Sammy. I miss him too."

He leaned over the backseat and I leaned forward. We hugged awkwardly then I climbed out of the car.

Later that night I had part two of my family reconciliation when

Mom came into my room. I had been lying on my single bed—the bunk beds now gone—looking through the journal with all the Levels but closed it quickly when I heard her coming. I put my face into the pillow and pretended to be sleeping. I knew it was her because she sat on the bed and started rubbing my back, just like she always did to Sammy.

"Cal," she said. "I heard about your talk with your father. I wanted to come and tell you I'm sorry too. We shouldn't have been yelling."

I continued to pretend to be asleep.

"I think it's a good idea for us all to see the counsellor. Me included. We're struggling with everything and it will help if we struggle together. I know I've been hard on you but I—"

"And hard on Dad," I said.

She paused. "Yes, and hard on Dad. But I'm going to try my best to let things go. I have to realize that everyone grieves in their own way and it's not fair for me to expect you two to want to do everything I do. Anyway, I'm happy we're going to talk to someone."

Her arms wrapped around me from behind and I turned. We hugged and I whispered, "I'm sorry I told you I wanted you to leave."

"I know," she whispered back.

CHAPTER 41

WINTER GAVE WAY TO SPRING AND A WARM BREEZE BLEW through the open kitchen door. The snow was gone except for a few shadowy places and everywhere the world was starting to green again. The birds were back. Soon the corn would be planted and I could start judging the passage of time by its height. Summer was around the corner.

I was lying in bed listening to a sparrow outside when something caught my attention. I climbed from my bed and went to the window to get a closer look. When I was sure of what I'd seen I raced downstairs.

"Mom, Dad!" I yelled.

Mom was sitting at the kitchen table and stood up quickly. "What is it, Cal?" she said, looking frightened.

I heard footsteps racing down the stairs after me and Dad appeared in his pajamas. "Cal?" he said. "What's the problem?"

I ran over and grabbed his hand. "Come quickly—outside!"

I pulled him through the screen door and Mom followed. We rounded the house to my bedroom window. In front of it stood the two cherry trees—Sakura and Big Tree.

"Look," I said, pulling down the lowest branch from Sakura.

They got closer to see.

Sure enough, there they were—tiny miracles on every branch.

"Sammy!" I said.

The whole branch was covered in them. Tiny buds, some already showing signs of opening. I looked over at Big Tree—it had buds too, but that was no surprise, it had blossomed every spring since we'd moved to Huxbury, but Sakura, well, that was Sammy.

Dad looked at Mom and smiled. She wrapped her arms around his waist and smiled too.

I didn't stay long to admire the tree. I had something else I needed to do. I raced back inside and grabbed my backpack from my room then sprinted across our lawn toward the fields.

"Where are you going?" Mom called after me.

"I have something I need to do!" I yelled back.

By the time I arrived at Aleta's house I was completely out of breath and my legs were tired. I leaned against the front door and knocked. Raquel opened it and I practically fell on top of her.

"Is...Aleta...here?" I panted.

Raquel raised her eyebrows. "She's upstairs. Is everything all right?"

"Everything's fine," I said.

When I entered Aleta's room she looked at me like I was a ghost.

"Cal?"

I realized I hadn't even knocked.

She was wearing sweatpants and a tank top. A book lay open on her chest.

I tossed my backpack next to her on the bed.

"I'm ready," I said.

For a second she looked confused then she smiled and put her book on the bedside table. As she stood up she said, “Are you sure?”

I nodded.

“Okay, let’s go.”

The air was chilly but the sun was warm as we walked through the fields to our Secret Spot. When we got there we stood in front of the trees for a moment, just staring. The place looked the same from the outside but when we entered it felt different. The forest was quieter, like all the spring sparrows had decided to stop singing at once, and the decaying leaves underneath our feet were soft and soundless.

On the far side of the forest we stood staring out over the spring-touched landscape. Lake Huron shimmered its familiar gold and blue in the distance. Tiny patches of snow lay hidden beside trees and hills but everywhere else the world was awakening. A small gust of wind picked up and the landscape changed. The trees bent and waved while the young grass danced in unison.

I looked at Aleta beside me. She was just as lost in the moment as I was. I reached my hand and found hers and she wrapped her fingers around mine.

In my head I heard Oliver’s words as I watched a hawk soaring above.

I am the thousand winds that blow,

I am the diamond glints on snow,

Then there was Sammy’s voice, a whisper in the maples. *It’s so beautiful, Cal.*

I breathed in long and hard. “Yes, Sammy, it is.”

I walked back into the forest and found a comfortable root to sit on. From my backpack I grabbed the journal and a pen. I began flipping through the pages, looking at each picture and reading the inscriptions below.

These will be my guide, I thought.

I traced the last drawing with my finger—an eagle in gold pencil crayon—then flipped to a fresh page.

I stole a look at Aleta. She was sitting in her own maple chair, concentrating as she wrote in her journal. She looked up at me and smiled. I smiled back briefly, then began to write.

My name is Calvin Sinclair, I am eleven years old and this is a story about my brother.

ACKNOWLEDGEMENTS

To my friends and family who read this novel in its infancy and helped it grow—thank you. A special thanks to Wiz who has read this book as many times as I have, and to my mother who has supported my book as much as she has always supported me.

To Michelle Halket, for taking these words and transforming them into a novel. Without you, this story would exist only on my computer and in a much poorer state.

And to my wonderful wife and children—you are the most important part of my life—thank you for being so patient with my writing. I love you.

Alex Lyttle is a pediatrician living in Calgary, Alberta with his wife and three children. He was raised in London, Ontario—the setting of his first novel, *From Ant to Eagle*, which he wrote based on his experiences working in the Pediatric Oncology unit.

When he is not working, writing or playing basketball, he enjoys learning new magic tricks to perform for his young patients.

Catch up with him at alexlyttle.com.

DISCUSSION QUESTIONS

1. What do you believe is the central theme of the novel?

2. How would you describe Sammy and Cal's relationship before Cal meets Aleta?

3. Why does Dr. Parker do magic tricks? What is it that Cal learns from Dr. Parker and Oliver that helps him relate better to his brother?

4. Why did Oliver choose to read the poem at the funeral? What do you feel about his version of heaven?

5. Everyone deals with the death of a loved one differently. Discuss the contrast between the various characters' methods for dealing with loss, (e.g. Cal and his parents, Aleta and her father and sister.)

6. Did you want the novel to end differently? If so, how?

INTERVIEW WITH ALEX LYTTLE

How much of From Ant to Eagle is based on your real experiences as a pediatrician and how much did you make up?

It is no secret that there is as much truth in this novel as there is fiction. I began writing the novel during my oncology rotation in medical school and wrote as a form of catharsis. Many of the characters are drawn from real patients—their names and ages changed for confidentiality reasons. Sammy and Cal are not based on specific people, but instead, are a combination of various people. Pieces of their relationship are also drawn from my relationship with my younger brother. The levels, the love of *Goosebumps* books, and—as the amazing Andrew Norriss put it, "the casual brutality of their relationship"—are all experiences I shared with my brother, for better or for worse.

Between medicine and parenting, how did you find time to write?

During the seven years it took me to write this novel, I also got married, had/raised three children, wrote two medical board exams, and worked long hours as a pediatric resident. So the obvious question is: where did I find the time? Clearly it wasn't easy—it took seven years after all—but the truth is, if you love something enough, you will find time to do it. For me, writing wasn't something I needed to make time for, it was something I obsessively did. Between diaper changes and playing with the kids, between 24-hour call shifts and studying, I always found a few minutes here and there to write. If you aspire to write your own novel, I encourage you to not wait. There will always be other things going on, but if you start now, and find that you truly enjoy it, the time will find you.

This is a sad novel; did you set out to make it that way or did it just evolve into that?

When I started writing *From Ant to Eagle* I had only two ideas—to write about brothers and to write about the effect cancer has on siblings. I didn't know how it would end, or even how it would begin, I just started writing. Over the course of the next seven years, it evolved into what it is today. In the end, I hope that people will not read this novel and think of it as a "sad novel" but instead, a love story. Because to me, the central theme of this novel is not loss or death, but love; the love that exists between brothers, even if it is not always evident.

Did you ever consider writing the novel so that Sammy didn't die?

When I began sending my novel out to literary agents, I heard back from the very first agent I sent it to. She said, "I love the novel, I think it has wonderful potential, but I think you should consider rewriting the ending so that Sammy doesn't die." So I did exactly that. I rewrote the second half of the novel and made it so that Sammy lived (he got a bone marrow transplant and Cal was his donor). But after rereading it, I decided it no longer felt like my novel. Yes, it was happier, and yes, many people would likely prefer it that way, but it wasn't what I had set out to write. The harsh reality of pediatric oncology is that there are thousands of children like Sammy and Cal out there, and in the end, I chose to tell their story.

What's up next for you and your writing career?

Right now, I am working on a middle grade, fantasy novel in which animals talk, one girl has supernatural powers, and nobody has cancer. It is a respite from the last novel. I will eventually write another book like it—in fact, I already have most of it written in my head—however I suspect it will be years before I finally get it on paper.